IRISH
ALIBI

ALSO BY RALPH McINERNY

IRISH ALIBI

RALPH McINERNY

 St. Martin's Minotaur New York

IRISH ALIBI. Copyright © 2007 by Ralph McInerny. All rights reserved. Printed in the United States of America. No part of this book may be used or reproduced in any manner whatsoever without written permission except in the case of brief quotations embodied in critical articles or reviews. For information, address St. Martin's Press, 175 Fifth Avenue, New York, N.Y. 10010.

www.minotaurbooks.com

Library of Congress Cataloging-in-Publication Data

McInerny, Ralph M.
   Irish alibi / Ralph McInerny.—1st ed.
      p. cm.
   ISBN-13: 978-0-312-36457-1
   ISBN-10: 0-312-36457-1
   1. Knight, Roger (Fictitious character)—Fiction.   2. Knight, Philip (Fictitious character)—Fiction.   3. College teachers—Indiana—South Bend—Fiction.   4. Private investigators—Indiana—South Bend—Fiction.   5. University of Notre Dame—Fiction.   6. South Bend (Ind.)—Fiction.   7. United States—History—Civil War, 1861–1865—Influence—Fiction.   8. Murder—Investigation—Fiction.   9. College stories.   I. Title.

PS3563.A31166I63 2007
813'.54—dc22
                                                          2007018142

First Edition: September 2007

10 9 8 7 6 5 4 3 2 1

For Lynn and Alasdair

We are but pilgrims, and the skin
That covers us, the tent wherein
Awake or sleeping, we abide
Till death a dwelling-place provide.

—John Bannister Tabb

PART ONE

1

THE HUGE FACADE OF THE HES-
burgh Library is visible to fans in the
Notre Dame stadium, particularly those on the south end, and,
of course, to the millions watching on television. On it, Christ
the Teacher lifts his arms in a way that has led the irreverent
to refer to Him as "Touchdown Jesus." Foes of Notre Dame
will not be convinced that this designation sprang up sponta-
neously and was nurtured and broadcast by perfervid sports
commentators. Critics see in this yet another instance of a
woeful mingling of the secular and sacred on the South Bend
campus, with football elevated almost to the status of a liturgi-
cal rite. Of course the mural must have been designed with
this in view.

Some errors are interesting, and perhaps this is one of
them. The theologically illiterate have even been known to
object to the bumper-sticker legend GOD MADE NOTRE
DAME #1. But who would imagine this to refer to the football
team rather than to Our Lady Theotokos? It is of course otherwise with the illuminated number 1 atop Grace Hall, outlined
against the blue-gray autumnal sky. This glowing numeral
shines brightly through good seasons and bad, unaffected by
the actual ranking of the Fighting Irish. To the skeptic, this

electrified hubris is on a par with the huge statue of Moses on the east side of the library, arm raised, one imperious digit thrust upward. How does one see this as different from the illuminated sign? And then, of course, there is "Fair Catch" Corby.

Father William Corby was one of the priests of Notre Dame who went off to the Civil War as a chaplain, attached to the famous Irish Brigade from New York. He was at Gettysburg and before that bloody battle gave general absolution to the troops, so many of whom were about to meet their Maker. The event is commemorated on that battlefield by a statue of Corby blessing the Irish Brigade. The twin of the statue stands before Corby Hall on campus. The hand raised in absolution, like the finger of Moses, like the uplifted arms of Christ the Teacher, has received an athletic interpretation, as if the intrepid priest, who went on to become president of the university, were indeed signaling for a fair catch.

These items of Notre Dame lore formed the heart of the book *Irish Icons*, copies of which were being signed by its author, Magnus O'Toole, in the campus bookstore just hours before the game with Georgia Tech. It has been said that anything not nailed down can be sold on game day to the thousands of faithful fans who converge on Notre Dame, filling local motels whose rates have tripled, even quadrupled, for the occasion. Cars come bumper to bumper along the Indiana Toll Road from east and west; they descend southward and ascend northward on the Jacob's ladder of U.S. 31; they come as well on lesser modes of access known to the initiate. For days before a game, private planes descend on the Michiana Airport, taking their turn in the landing pattern with commercial flights whose seats have been reserved for months. Scattered about the campus are fragrant charcoal fires on which hamburgers and brats send up propitiatory smoke as if invoking divine patronage for the team. Crowds move about the campus in the hours before the game, marveling at the beauty of the grounds and the majesty of the buildings. The devout kneel at the Grotto or pay a visit to Sacred Heart Basilica. Others stand as if mesmerized by the great golden dome atop the Main Building on which Mary, the patroness of the university, gazes serenely southward. Seasons come and go; coaches rise and fall; players and students are quadrennially replaced as if in some metaphor of the ages of man. She has seen it all so many times. *Sub specie aeternitatis*, as it were.

And in the bookstore, Magnus O'Toole was doing a land-office business autographing his book for eager purchasers, many of whom regarded it as a souvenir rather than as something to be read. Their decision perhaps may be the wiser.

He sat at a table on which copies of his book were piled, but, given his small stature, he might as well have been standing. Beneath his tweed jacket, he wore a green turtleneck. As he scrawled his name in book after book, he seemed to flash his Notre Dame ring, Class of 1977, like a proud girl displaying her diamond. His beard exaggerated his fixed smile. The occasion was successful beyond the dreams of avarice, and this despite the formidable competition. At other tables other books were being bought and signed by their authors. Gerry Faust, who had sold his soul to Notre Dame, a bargain not exactly reciprocated, was there, of course. Regis Philbin was hawking a DVD on which his singing was mercifully eclipsed

5

by a chorus. Monk Molloy was signing a book made up of his otherwise unmemorable presidential addresses. For Magnus to prosper in such a setting was success indeed. Two bookstore minions kept the line moving and replenished the supply of books. Magnus was ecstatic.

"Magnus, you old crook."

The startled author looked up. A hand was thrust at him, and then faulty recognition shone in his bloodshot eyes. He shook the hand of a classmate, trying desperately to remember his name.

"Basil?"

"Quintin. Quintin Kelly." A frown came and went before this correction was made.

"Alumni Hall."

"Dillon."

Well, it had been years since the two men had seen one another, and Kelly had the advantage, as Magnus's name was prominent in forty-point type beneath the flattering photograph on the poster propped behind the signing table.

"How long will you be here?" Kelly asked.

A bookstore assistant pointed to the poster. Magnus's allotted two hours had twenty minutes to go.

"I'll wait for you outside."

"Do you want a book?"

"Later."

"That may be too late."

Shamed into a purchase, Kelly took the autographed book and sidled through the crowd to a doorway. Resentment at not being recognized by his old classmate came and went. Would he have recognized O'Toole without the help of that poster? Outside, he took a package of Pall Malls from his jacket pocket and inserted one between his thin lips. Before lighting it, he looked out toward the parking lot as if a firing squad had been mustered there. He might be waiting to be blindfolded. Then he lit his cigarette and drew smoke into his wheezing lungs. This was his first return to campus in twenty years.

2 IN THEIR APARTMENT IN ONE OF the hundred and more villas that make up graduate student housing east of the library, the Knight brothers, Roger and Philip, were at table enjoying a pregame brunch.

"What a crock," Phil said, closing a copy of *Irish Icons*.

"Why did you buy it?"

"I didn't. It was sent to you. Inscribed." He pushed the book toward his younger brother.

There is obesity and obesity, and Roger's enormous bulk suggested virtue rather than vice, as if God meant him to weigh three hundred pounds and anything less would be a flaw in the providential plan. The Huneker Professor of Catholic Studies took up the book his brother slid toward him and opened the cover. He read aloud.

" 'To a fellow much-admired author. Magnus O'Toole.' "

Roger smiled at the self-referential inscription. "Does that mean he actually read my monograph on Baron Corvo?"

"Another nonbook."

"Mine?"

"That."

"When did it come?"

"Half an hour ago. You were still in the shower. Hand delivered."

"By the author?"

"He said he was in your class. A kid named Lanier."

"Ah. Caleb." But the smile of recognition faded. "Why would he have brought it?"

"To get rid of it?"

Roger had begun to leaf through the book, half-murmuring sentences as he went. "He has been badly served by his translator."

"O'Toole is a sportswriter from Atlanta."

Roger looked at his brother. Phil might have been the After to his Before in a weight-loss ad, except that he was several heads taller. "How did you know that?"

"Read the dust jacket."

Roger fell back in his chair, repeating the phrase. "Dust jacket. Dust jacket. An expressive phrase. As the body clothes the soul."

"You sound like a sportswriter."

Roger returned to the book, holding it open on the table with a huge and pudgy hand. He read in silence for a moment. "He's got Corby all wrong."

"How so?"

"He seems to think he was with the Confederate army."

"Didn't he bless both Southern and Northern armies?"

"I'm sure that was his intention."

Phil stood, stretched, and touched the ceiling with his fingertips. "Sure you don't want to go to the game, Roger?"

"Not today. I'll be preparing dinner. Be sure to bring Father Carmody back with you."

Caleb ran back to the car after putting his uncle's book into Philip Knight's hand and hopped into the passenger seat. At the wheel, Sarah Kincade looked at him, waiting. "Well?"

"What?"

"What did the great man say?"

"I gave it to his brother. And don't knock Roger Knight until you've had a class with him."

"I think of him as a rival."

"Let's go."

"We should have walked."

As Sarah returned her car to a student parking lot, negotiating several checkpoints that kept the unauthorized off campus, Caleb tried to feel satisfaction about fulfilling his Uncle Magnus's request. He had gone to Atlanta during the midterm break, wanting to see the sites he was hearing about in class, and had babbled on and on to his uncle about the course he was taking from Roger Knight.

"Notre Dame and the Civil War?" Magnus had asked. "What kind of a course is that?"

Magnus became excited as Caleb described the course—no surprise there. Since settling in Atlanta after a stint in the marines, Magnus had become a member of that passionate species, the adopted Southerner. He had read all three volumes of Shelby Foote, all four of Allan Nevins, and the three of Bruce Catton. His apartment was stuffed with other books on the Civil War. An accent few would have ackowledged as Southern had altered his Minnesota dialect. He had succumbed to what Roger Knight had called that most seductive allegiance, a lost cause.

"That goddamn Sherman," Magnus drawled.

Caleb cut short his account of Roger Knight's class. What would his uncle make of the fact that General Sherman's boys had attended Notre Dame during the War Between the States and that the general had been feted on campus after Appomattox?

The great fascination for Caleb of Roger Knight's class was the way the past was brought alive and surprising connections with Notre Dame brought out. With the zeal of a convert, Caleb had decided to write an article on General Sherman and Notre Dame for an alternative student paper. Because Roger Knight had mentioned that one of Sherman's sons had died while visiting his father during the siege of Vicksburg and another had died at Notre Dame and been buried in Cedar Grove Cemetery on campus, Caleb had taken Sarah on a tour of the place in an unsuccessful effort to find the boy's grave.

"Oh, he was moved after the war," Roger said. "I should have mentioned that. Not that a visit to Cedar Grove is ever a waste of time. You must have noticed that great plinth marking the site of Alexis Coquillard's grave?"

"Who was he?"

Like most students, Caleb had come to Notre Dame historically illiterate. His knowledge of the past of Western civilization was hazy; even the events that had taken place on the

North American continent during the past three hundred years were more or less a closed book to him. How then could he have imagined that the university to which he came had such a fascinating past? In Atlanta, he switched the topic of conversation to this broader and safer avenue.

"Is he a historian?"

"Roger Knight? No, his doctorate is in philosophy."

"Good God."

Caleb had already heard all he wanted to hear of his uncle's long-ago travails in philosophy courses at Notre Dame, although his reenactment of a lecture on the intuition of being was quite the performance.

"Tell me about your book."

It sounded like a dozen other books for sale in the campus bookstore, but there seemed to be an insatiable appetite for them.

"Maybe I should have used a pen name."

Was it that bad? "Why?"

Magnus grew pensive. However thoroughly transplanted he had become, Uncle Magnus's athletic allegiance was to his alma mater, not the highest recommendation in Atlanta, where he covered Georgia and Georgia Tech with some semblance of enthusiasm. But his fundamental loyalty emerged whenever Notre Dame faced Georgia Tech, and Magnus was the object of pointed jibes from his fellow sportswriters and the recipient of irate and threatening e-mails.

And now, just in time for the big contest between Notre Dame and Georgia Tech, *Irish Icons* had been published, and his uncle had been scheduled to autograph copies in the campus bookstore before the game.

In the Atlanta airport, waiting for his flight back to South Bend, Caleb had called his mother in Minneapolis to report on his visit to her brother.

"Why didn't Magnus ever marry?"

"Who said he didn't?"

"What happened?"

"Ask him."

They parked and locked Sarah's car and then began to walk in the direction of music. The Notre Dame band was making its traditional circuit of the campus before heading for the stadium.

Before leaving, Magnus autographed every book on the table and then pushed back, thanking Jonathon, the clerk who had overseen his signing.

"I think I did pretty well."

Jonathon nodded. Every author did well on a game day signing.

Restored to anonymity, Magnus elbowed his way through the crowd to the door. Outside Quintin Kelly was waiting. Magnus stared at him.

"You're smoking!"

"That's what happens when you light a cigarette."

The aroma of secondhand smoke was overpoweringly attractive. "Can I have one of those?"

"This is a smoke-free campus."

"Come on." The autumn air was clouded with smoke and sweetened by the smell of burning charcoal. Quintin shook a cigarette free and extended it to Magnus. Magnus's hand moved toward it, then stopped. Thus had Adam hesitated when Eve offered him an apple. He decided to follow Oscar Wilde's advice. The only way to get rid of temptation is to succumb to it. He inhaled and a wave of dizziness swept momentarily over him.

"You got a ticket, Quintin?"

"I bought one from a scalper for a hundred dollars."

"A bargain. Want to join me in the press box?"

"Are you serious?"

"Of course."

"Let me see if I can sell this ticket."

Quintin realized a 50 percent profit on his investment, and they headed toward the stadium.

"My secretary," Magnus explained when the guard squinted at Quintin.

Quintin drew a hand up his sleeve. "My shorthand."

Inside they had to wait for the elevator, but soon they were rising in the car, which was crammed cheek by jowl with denizens of the press. The door opened onto a large area with a bar that was doing a brisk business. Magnus ordered a Bloody Mary for himself, another for his guest, and then led Quintin to his assigned place in the front row of the banked seats. Below them the field gleamed greenly as if it were an aerial photo. The stands were already almost full; the visiting band was being ignored by nearly eighty thousand fans.

14

"What a view," Quintin said. "Am I glad I ran into you."

As if to establish equity, he put his copy of *Irish Icons* on the surface before him. Magnus had taken a portable computer from his shoulder bag and was getting ready. The press box was equipped for wireless, and he was soon linked with the city room in Atlanta. A face appeared on his screen and began to speak. A technical exchange went on for several minutes, and Quintin looked out over the field. He was beginning to wonder if he wanted to have the conversation with Magnus he had come all this way for.

Over the next hours, Magnus was busy tapping out a running commentary on the game that unfolded below them, a blur of prose that would be shaped into something resembling English by a rewrite man in Atlanta. Georgia Tech scored within the first five minutes, but it proved to be their only points of the game. The Irish ran up the score until the third quarter and then sent in the second team. Third-stringers were playing before it was over.

Magnus and Quintin had had another drink at halftime and had another before going down in the elevator. Outside, Quintin offered Magnus a cigarette, and he took it eagerly.

"My wife smokes," he said.

"I know."

After the game, Caleb and Sarah went to Legends, the senior bar, which was senior indeed for the occasion, jammed full of alumni trying to communicate above the general din. It was impossible to get within ordering distance of the bar, so they borrowed bottles from a table whose occupants were replaying the game, designing plays on paper napkins, making body movements from a seated position meant to indicate what they would have had the linemen do.

"Another round," a playmaker said when Caleb removed two bottles from the trove in the center of the table.

"Coming up."

"Let's go outside, for heaven's sake," Sarah said.

When they were leaving, they ran into Uncle Magnus entering.

"Caleb!" But Magnus's eyes were approvingly on Sarah.

"You'll die of thirst in here," Caleb said.

"Is there somewhere else?"

"I have an idea."

Magnus introduced them to his classmate Quintin Kelly. The two older men did not seem in need of more drink, but Magnus took the beer from Caleb's hand. Sarah gave hers to Kelly, who tried to pay her for it.

"It's all right. We stole them."

"Ho ho."

Truth is seldom believed. The benches that lined the walk-ways were filled with fans; others were seated on the ledge around the reflecting pool in front of the library. In the gloam-ing, Canada geese stared beadily at these invaders of their turf.

"Where are we going?" Sarah asked Caleb.

"It's a surprise."

"Oh, no."

"Tell me about Sarah," Magnus said, taking her arm.

"Have you been smoking?"

"I quit."

"You smell of tobacco."

He pointed. "Quintin smokes." He paused. "So does my wife."

He let go of her arm and joined Quintin. "What did you mean, you know?"

"I don't follow you."

"You said you knew my wife smokes."

"A lucky guess."

3   SARAH KINCADE WAS A DAUGHTER
of Memphis whose family could be
traced back to the original colony of Virginia. An ancestor had
been a senator from Mississippi whose seat had subsequently
been filled by the sainted Jefferson Davis. On her mother's
side, she was related to a member of the cabinet of the Confederacy. But it was not these political appointments that were
the pride of the family. So many potential forebears had fallen
in battle during the War Between the States that it seemed a
miracle that the family had continued. But it had, prouder in
defeat than it ever could have been in victory, its vast land-
holdings intact when the smoke of battle cleared. During the
horrors of Reconstruction, the Kincades had persisted in
pride and honor, no matter the carpetbagger who lay under a
stone a hundred yards from the ancestral home—a stone on
which had been chiseled *Sic semper tyrannis*. The Kincades
had retained their Catholic faith with something of the tenac-
ity of the English recusants. John Bannister Tabb, the priest-
poet, had been a family friend.

Over the years, land had been sold but the huge house
overlooking the river retained, as well as the home in Memphis where Sarah had been raised. Her father had been the

first Kincade to go north to Notre Dame to school, and a tradition seemed established when her twin brothers, Malcolm and Eugene, now juniors, went off to South Bend. It was their experience that overcame her father's reluctance to send Sarah to what he still thought of as an all-male university. In her freshman year, she had met Caleb.

"Lanier?"

He spelled it for her.

"I know how it's spelled. Are you related to Sidney?"

The question drew a blank. No matter. His expression when he puzzled over her question caused his hitherto ordinary face to morph into the countenance of the ideal male she knew she was destined for. She had read Trollope's *Ayala's Angel*, and it might have been constructed from entries in the diary she had kept locked in a drawer of her bedroom desk. She felt she knew now why she had come to Notre Dame.

Caleb seemed unaware that fate, nay, providence, had brought them together, but even that unawareness was attractive to her.

The honors class they were both taking in their freshman year was a bore, but what is more binding than a shared discontent? Caleb was also taking a course from Roger Knight and acquired a standard for the appraisal of professors.

"But his reputation is all hearsay," Sarah said.

Caleb shook his head. "I talked him into a late enrollment. I'm in his class."

"When did you talk to him?" Her lower lip puffed out in an almost pout, and she widened her great gray eyes. Confederate gray. When she tossed her head, her long single braid bounced between her shoulders. She was half annoyed that she was not privy to all his actions.

"You can get into the class if you act fast."

"What is it?"

"Notre Dame and the Civil War."

Sarah said nothing. Their relationship had prospered because she had resolutely kept her proud ancestry offstage. Much as she was attracted to Caleb, certain as she was that he was her destiny and she was his, she did not dare risk providing him the occasion of making some unforgivable remark about the South. Her ears had already been offended by condescending remarks from students for whom the South meant only Florida and mindless hours in the sun.

"Sounds interesting."

"I know nothing about the Civil War."

"It's a vast subject."

"Why don't you sign up for the course?"

She put a hand on his arm. "I find it difficult to pay attention when you're in the room."

He actually looked away, then turned back to her. "Cut it out." But his voice had softened. She touched the cleft in his chin.

"What's wrong?" He rubbed at his chin, then looked at his hand.

"It's still there."

What she loved about him was the fact that he always thought she was kidding when she practically threw herself at him. They had so much fun together, but it was not a contact sport. Just buddies, that seemed to be his view of it. Sarah was patient, though; how could she not be, occupying as she did a providential role? Then he had confided in her his intention to write an article on General Sherman and Notre Dame.

"Do you think you should?"

"It's a fascinating topic."

"But so controversial!"

"Controversial?"

How could she explain to him that the war that had once divided the country might prove to be a wedge between them? Her apprehension lifted when he put his arm about her.

"The Civil War ended in 1865, Sarah. It's ancient history."

He really believed that.

It was while she was agonizing over the wisdom of introducing Caleb to her brothers that he met them without any intervention on her part. They confronted one another when their teams met in interhall football. In the final minutes of the game, Caleb caught an uncatchable ball and fell across the goal line for the winning score. Eugene, who had unsuccessfully defended on the play, helped Caleb to his feet. The two walked side by side off the field and were joined by Malcolm, who shook Caleb's hand. Sarah was filled with tenderness at the sight of her two burly redheaded brothers looking like bookends, each with an arm around Caleb's broad shoulders. It was all in the tradition of honorable conflict, noblesse oblige, the family's tradition and that of the old Confederacy.

She had read of how opposing troops had exchanged banter throughout the night before a battle. She joined the trio as they returned to their halls with their teams.

"Our sister, Sarah," Eugene said. "What's your name, Yank?"

So it was her identical twin brothers who introduced her to Caleb, or thought they had. Neither she nor Caleb corrected their impression. Sarah had noticed the use of "Yank." Though spoken in a friendly way, the word held the promise of enmity.

Later, Caleb admitted that at least when her brothers were in uniform he could tell them apart. Because of the numbers.

Caleb had told her of his visit to his uncle in Atlanta, and meeting the adopted Southerner was a bonus of the evening. When Magnus left her side to join his classmate, she said to Caleb, "I know where you're taking us."

"It's a surprise for Magnus."

At the door of the Knights' apartment, the four of them stood in the gathering dark, waiting for the bell to be answered.

"Who lives here?" Magnus asked.

"One of my professors."

Quintin groaned.

"A fellow author," Sarah said. Caleb had read the inscription his uncle had written in the book he wanted put into Roger Knight's hands.

And then the door opened and the huge figure of Roger

Knight, or a significant portion of it, was framed in the doorway, silhouetted against the light from within.

"Caleb," he cried. "And who have we here?"

Introductions were made as they entered. Philip was the tall brother, Father Carmody the priest.

4 FORTIFIED WITH THE DRINKS HE'D had in the press box, along with the beer Caleb had given him, Magnus rose to hitherto unachieved conversational heights during the next few hours spent in the apartment of the Knight brothers. Even Father Carmody seemed interested.

First of all, there was Roger, a blimp of a man, but for all that everything Caleb had claimed, and more. Roger seemed surprised that Magnus had actually read his monograph on Baron Corvo.

"Had you ever heard of him while you were at Notre Dame?"

"Did you know Richard Sullivan?"

"Only by reputation."

"He was a member of the English department during the golden years. Stories, novels, but above all his book on Notre Dame."

"I know that, of course."

"All the royalties went to the university. There was a true Notre Dame man."

"My royalties from Corvo would not have added much to the current affluence."

There was a topic that Magnus could have run with. Like most alumni, he was at once overwhelmed and slightly repelled by the visible wealth the university had come into since his days on campus. It is difficult for anyone other than a Franciscan to sing the praises of poverty, and Magnus was himself anything but an unworldly man, but the conspicuous signs of wealth that had transformed the Notre Dame campus struck him as out of keeping with any effort to convey to students that they had here no lasting city.

He had just prompted a reaction from Roger to *Irish Icons* when Philip Knight asked Magnus what he had thought of the game. Switching gears with the ease granted him by the alcohol he had consumed, Magnus tipped back his head, looking up at Philip, and began pontificating on sports. Here he was an acknowledged expert, and in Philip Knight he had an interlocutor worthy of his steel.

"College sports have changed beyond recognition. Coaches are not shy to say that they are looking for recruits who want to play on Sundays. Future pros, that is. The campuses have become the minor leagues of the NFL."

"Was there interhall football when you were here?" the lovely Sarah asked.

"Yes. But no Bookstore Tournament!"

Sometimes an indirect answer is the best response. Magnus had taken no part in athletics during his time at Notre Dame. But then neither had Charlie Weis. Basketball or football, the point was that once young men who were students had engaged in sports in their spare time.

"When do athletes get a shot at an education nowadays?"

He reined himself in. He sounded too much like Jeremiah. And the truth was that he had delighted in the afternoon's contest and in Notre Dame's triumph over the visiting team. He only hoped his account would sound more neutral than he had felt while sending it in. Father Carmody detached himself from Caleb and joined them.

"What's this about student athletes?"

"I'm Magnus O'Toole, Father."

"I know."

Surely the priest wouldn't remember him as a student. "You've read my book?"

"I don't read anymore. Only re-read. You were here in the late seventies, '75, '76. . . ."

"1977!"

"My memory is going," the old priest said. "Writing that column for the *Observer* proved fateful, didn't it? Still with the *Constitution*?"

Magnus was delighted by the thought that his less than stellar career had been monitored on his old campus.

"It must be in the genes," Father Carmody said.

"How so?"

"Haven't you read your nephew's article on General Sherman and Notre Dame?"

"Caleb!" Magnus cried. "Come here. What's this about an article?"

Roger Knight produced the latest issue of the *Irish Rover*, opened to Caleb's article. Magnus took it and read it with moving lips.

"Wonderful, wonderful. Quintin, come here. Look at this."

He said to Father Carmody, "Quintin Kelly, Father. A class-mate."

The old priest peered at Quintin, who had large black eyes and olive skin and was bald in a way that had become fashionable. "You lived in Dillon. What are you doing now?"

Quentin seemed embarrassed with the priest, a reminder of his more orderly youth.

Magnus would have liked to hear Quentin's answer to Father Carmody's question—it occurred to him that he hadn't asked Quintin about himself—but Roger Knight had taken his arm.

"Would you like to see my modest Civil War collection?"

And off they went to the study, where Roger settled himself into a commodious wheeled chair and then began to move along the shelves, drawing Magnus's attention to what he had.

"Mathew Brady!"

Magnus opened a volume and began to leaf through it, studying the haunting photographs Brady had taken. "This must have been the first generation of the camera."

This earned him a little lecture on the transition from daguerreotype to photograph.

"Have you been through the tunnel that leads from the Morris Inn to the McKenna Center? The walls are lined with old photographs of this place."

"I didn't know there was a tunnel."

Roger smiled. "It's not a heating tunnel, you know. But there is a whole subterranean network of heating tunnels beneath the campus. They were featured in one of the Father Dowling mysteries."

"I've never heard of them."

"Are you a native of the South?"

"I was raised in Minneapolis."

"I've been trying to place your accent."

"I see you have Shelby Foote."

"Oh yes. Always a Confederate spin, but delightful reading."

Later Magnus was elated to learn that Sarah was from Memphis and from a great Southern family.

"The Kincades," he repeated, letting his lids drop in recognition.

"When Caleb told me his name was Lanier, you can imagine what I thought."

And so they commemorated Sidney Lanier, raising a bumper of merlot to the memory of the writer.

"And how long have you been in Atlanta?"

"I feel I was born there."

"Honestly, whenever I'm in Atlanta, I feel I'm"—she looked around, then leaned toward him and whispered—"in a Northern city."

Magnus knew what she meant. He would infinitely rather be in some such place as Savannah or Charleston or, for that matter, Memphis, all of them unequivocally Southern. Sarah was right, Atlanta had changed, and you could name all the streets Peachtree and it wouldn't disguise it. In the parish where he didn't go to Mass, there had been an influx of New Englanders, along with well-paying jobs in the electronics industry they had brought with them. The pastor, too, was an import who sounded like someone imitating JFK.

"Is Mrs. O'Toole with you?" Sarah asked.

"Not this trip. How long have you known Caleb?"

"Oh, we're old friends."

Magnus did not lift his hand in benediction, though he certainly wanted to. A sudden wave of sadness swept over him, and he had a momentary vision of the contrast between a couple's hopeful beginnings and the reality of their future. Sarah had asked about Mrs. O'Toole. Mimi would never answer to that. For that matter, she no longer answered to Mimi.

"Call me Madeline, for God's sake."

And not Madeline O'Toole, either. She found his family name comic. She published her novels under the pen name Madeline Butler.

5 ⟶ FROM THE KNIGHTS' APARTMENT,
Magnus and Quintin followed a diagonal though not particularly straight line across the campus to the Morris Inn.

"You got into the Morris Inn on a game day!" Quintin stopped walking as he said this, though he seemed to continue to move in place.

"No, no. My car is in the lot there."

"Where are we going?"

"Let's check out the Morris Inn first."

They checked out the Morris Inn. They ended in the great tent erected behind the hotel to accommodate the influx of thirsty fans. Magnus seemed surprised that the temporary bar did not have single malt scotch.

"Give me something domestic, then."

They found an outside table, and Magnus lifted his glass to the starry heavens above. He was filled with euphoria. His return to his alma mater had been, if he said so himself, a triumph. He had sold a lot of books; he had watched a Notre Dame victory; he had met the much touted Roger Knight as well as the Southern belle who seemed so attached to his nephew Caleb. Once more he felt a fleeting sadness. But who would not be immobilized if he knew the future?

"I didn't realize for some time that Madeline was your wife."

Quintin's statement came accompanied by background noise—other conversations, music, the constant coming and going of festive fans—and was apparently part of a narrative he had begun while Magnus was studying the sky. He lowered his gaze and looked at Quintin with both eyes.

"You know Madeline?"

"As Madeline Butler. She's one of my authors."

"Your authors?"

Quintin Kelly, it emerged, owned the publishing house in Athens, Georgia, that brought out the gaudy paperbacks Madeline wrote and Magnus considered a travesty. Madeline had invoked *Gone with the Wind* as her model.

"The O'Haras were Catholic!" Magnus had responded. It seemed a time for irrelevancies.

"You're just jealous."

"Of course I'm jealous." She knew his dream of writing a real book rather than the ephemeral column on the sports page, where like all his ilk he affected omniscience and turned athletics into an accountant's nightmare, a blur of statistics. And all along Madeline had been nursing the dream of becoming the successor of Margaret Mitchell. (Another Catholic, by the way, of sorts.)

"What does that have to do with anything?"

That first quarrel had been occasioned by her first novel.

She presented it to him like an illegitimate child. He had no idea that she had written it, let alone found a publisher, and here it was, a bulky paperback on whose cover some demanding position from the Kama Sutra seemed illustrated.

He got over it, more or less. After all, why should he be threatened by a piece of schlock like this? But *Passion's Dregs* was followed by *Maid in Vicksburg* and *Dancing in Charleston.* They were shameless exploitations of the Civil War period, turning the great campaign into a crusade of concupiscence. With prosperity, Madeline rented an office in a high-rise near a suburban mall; she went off on writing vacations; she bought a beach house on Siesta Key. Magnus felt unmanned. They became estranged.

He had forgotten how beautiful she was, and the publicity photos used to promote her books came as almost a surprise. Her brunette hair framed her face; her eyes smoldered; her mouth seemed pursed for a kiss.

"You look like Vivien Leigh," he told her.

"The general's wife?"

It is odd to have to remember that you love your wife. And now a classmate he scarcely remembered was telling him that there was something going on between him and Madeline.

"I never made the connection," Quintin said, hunching over the table, which tilted under the pressure of his elbows. He lifted his glass high as if to preserve its contents in an unstable world. "Of course, she signed the contract Madeline O'Toole, but why was I supposed to think a Southern girl was married to you?"

"You sonofabitch."

Quintin ignored this. His expression was not unlike that of the counselor to whom Magnus and Madeline had taken their grievances. They had both loathed the smug marital negotiator who had looked blank when Magnus told him that marriage was a sacrament.

"For better or worse!"

"You can say that again," Madeline said.

But for the nonce, he and Madeline were on the same side, allied against this intruder. They could carry on their argument without a third party.

"We should have gone to a priest," Magnus said.

"That's what got us into this in the first place."

"We'll have children."

"No, we won't."

"Madeline, you're my wife."

"That's what's at issue."

She spoke now with the authority of commercial success. By comparison, he felt like a hack, his studied prose destined for the garbage dumps of Atlanta. How bitter to think now that he had written *Irish Icons* in an effort to establish parity with his wife.

"She wants to get an annulment," Quintin said.

"Over my dead body!"

"That's not necessary."

"Till death do us part. I'd fight it all the way to the Vatican."

"Magnus, you can't feel any worse about this than I do."

"That's what you think."

"I had no idea she had a husband, not at first."

Incredibly, Magnus found himself listening to Quintin recount how he had met Madeline, the week on Longboat Key, the rendezvous in Savannah.

"Savannah!"

"We wanted a neutral site."

"I want another drink."

"The bar is closed."

"We'll go to my place."

His place was a condo east of campus owned by the mega-corporation that owned the paper. Magnus drove with exaggerated caution, and they made it. He had a bottle of single malt scotch there, and as they opened it, Magnus had the odd thought that the two of them were conspiring against the collapse of Western civilization. He was developing this thought when he passed out.

6 PHIL DROVE FATHER CARMODY back to Holy Cross House, where the old priest lived, in the place, but not of it. It was there that priests of the Congregation of Holy Cross went when their careers were over and nothing lay ahead but the big exit. It was an exit many of them would not be aware of, their minds and memories having disembarked while the body continued the journey that would eventually end in the community cemetery along the road that connected Notre Dame and St. Mary's.

"How can you remember so many alumni, Father?"

"Most it would be hard to forget."

"He sent Roger a copy of his book."

"Kelly?"

"No, Magnus. Does Quintin Kelly write, too?"

"He tells me he's in publishing. Do people still read?"

They rounded the lake, and at the entrance of Holy Cross House, Father Carmody insisted that he needed no further help. Imagine coming into the place supported by Philip Knight. Everyone would assume that he was on the fast track to becoming gaga.

So it was a ramrod-straight, chin-uplifted Father Carmody

who sailed past the circular nurses' counter, giving a jaunty wave to the uniformed nurse, and continued down the corridor to his room. He did not turn on the light after he went in and shut the door. His windows gave him an unequaled view of the campus across the lake. He stood contemplating the scene of his youth and of most of his active years. The golden dome glowed in the night, and the giant statue of Our Lady—Notre Dame du Lac—above it. Through the trees, the lamps along the road seemed to twinkle in the movement of the branches, and the windows of buildings emitted little squares of light into the darkness. His throat constricted. He swallowed. He murmured a Memorare to the Lady on the dome, then sat, still wearing his jacket, and let the long long thoughts come.

What would he have made of himself now if he had been granted a prescient vision twenty, thirty years ago? Like most members of the Congregation still engaged in the daily tasks of the university, he would have regarded his confreres here across the lake as in the anteroom of eternity, living out their last days in bodies grown bent and twisted and aching, a vacant stare for visitors, or a little half smile in the hope of being recognized for what they once had been. It was that estimate of his present self that he rejected, and now, in the night, alone with God and the past, he could admit it was a species of pride. Why did he continue to insist that he was unlike the rest of men, an exception to the rule of the house, still vigorous and alive and caught up in the work of the university? By and large this was self-delusion, and looking with moist-eyed tenderness out his window, he could admit it.

Bah. He drove these thoughts away. He was becoming a

philosopher, that last refuge of the bewildered. He stood, started toward the light switch, but then stopped. Once more he sat, as if the night held thoughts that would only be driven away by light. Thank God for the Knight brothers. Bringing Roger to campus as the Huneker Professor of Catholic Studies had been among the final coups of Carmody's behind-the-scenes career at Notre Dame. A Philadelphia family with long connections with the university, now in a third generation drifted far from their youthful ideals, had been prompted to offer a propitiatory gift to Notre Dame—not that he had put it so baldly, but years in the game had taught him that generosity often springs from remorse—and the all but forgotten figure of Huneker had proved to be the hook on which to hang the benefaction.

"Who is Huneker?" he was asked while dining with representatives of three generations of the family and moving in for the kill.

"One of the first tasks of the occupant of your chair will be to bring Huneker to the attention of a new generation of Catholics."

Huneker's own ambiguous relation to the faith had made him seem an appropriate sponsor for this family's gift.

"Why not a memorial to a professor who taught us there?" the senior member of the family asked.

"Like?"

The old man's eyes roved in search of a memory. "Richard Sullivan?"

"Ah, Dick. Wonderful man. You had him in class?"

He had had him in class. He was allowed to reminisce

some more, and then, one more proof that the apparently contingent flux of events is governed by a wise providence, he recalled Sullivan's enthusiasm for Baron Corvo. Father Carmody plucked Roger Knight's monograph on that author from his bag and put it into the hands of the wise old man. Before they rose from the table, the deal had been struck. The money would be forthcoming, the chair would honor Huneker and be devoted to Catholic studies—a free variable not tied down to any department—and Father Carmody promised to secure Roger Knight as the first occupant of the chair.

And so he had gone to Rye to talk with Roger in the country retreat to which the two brothers had moved from Manhattan after Phil had been mugged for the third time. Phil was a private investigator who now took on only clients whose problems promised more than passing interest. His location did not matter; his office was notional rather than real: an 800 number contained in a quarter-page ad in the yellow pages of the directories of a few selected cities. Phil went where the work was, with Roger often in tow.

The size of the younger brother had given Father Carmody pause. There are fat people whose avoirdupois is carried as a temporary and shameful aberration and in whom the hope of slimming down to their putative natural size still flickers and will not die, however doomed to unfulfillment. Then there are those who, like Roger Knight, wear the enormity of their flesh as a destiny, an object of gentle self-mockery, to be sure, but for all that accepted, even celebrated. Father Carmody concluded that Roger was precisely the weight he ought to be. But could he be moved?

"The academic world was bad enough when I was a part of it, Father. It has only grown worse."

"We are talking of Notre Dame. Have you ever been there?"

"No."

"You will love it." He turned to Phil. "I need not mention that every sport in its season is played there."

Phil knew. He was already in his way a Subway alumnus, although, unlike Roger, he was not Catholic. Father Carmody devoted ten minutes to a brisk exchange of athletic information with Phil, then turned again to Roger.

"Tell me how you came into the Church."

"Sideways." A smile, but then he became serious.

Roger's story might have been Paul Claudel's or Jacques Maritain's a century earlier. If the outlook that dominated the academic world was true, if we were but random collections of electric charges, clusters of matter however complicated, destined to disintegrate without sequel, the individual human life would be by definition meaningless. But if life were indeed meaningless, men would not insist on developing theories that it is meaningless, thus granting it meaning of a sort. Such thoughts were the beginning. Roger's interest survived an unsatisfying visit to campus ministry; he read himself into the Church along a path Father Carmody had known many to follow: Chesterton, Belloc, C. S. Lewis, Josef Pieper.

"And of course Jacques Maritain."

"We have a Jacques Maritain Center, you know."

"I often consult its Web site."

It would be too much to say that the Web was what had

snared Roger Knight for Notre Dame, but it would be to say too little not to acknowledge the role of that virtual electronic world unknown to Father Carmody.

And so the Knights had come to Notre Dame. From time to time, Father Carmody had enlisted Philip's professional help to extricate the university from some potential embarrassment. He had become a frequent guest in the Knight apartment, his visits eased by the fact that Philip would come fetch him and take him back to Holy Cross House afterward. As he had done tonight.

Sitting in his room, which seemed gradually to have illumined as his eyes became accustomed to the darkness, Father Carmody thought of the little group that had gathered at the Knights' after the game. Magnus O'Toole, the stubby sportswriter whose beard seemed a mask rather than an adornment, had been full of the pride of authorship because of the little book he had cobbled together. But his deference to Roger had balanced this pardonable vanity. Magnus's nephew, Caleb, a fine boy, had been with a girl who clearly ranked their friendship higher than he did, Sarah Kincade. Her accent made Magnus's even more comical.

Kincade, Kincade. There had been Kincades at Notre Dame. Southerners of the deepest dye. A memory came, and with it a smile. Would it have been Sarah's father who had draped a huge piece of white canvas over the statue of Father Corby in protest against this indirect adulation of the Union cause? Discipline had been more than a word in those days, rules that were rigidly enforced rather than procedures with which to negotiate oneself out of a charge. Kincade had been lucky that he wasn't sent packing back to Memphis. Fortunately for him, Father Carmody had been there to intervene. He visited the prefect of discipline in his room, not his office.

"The rule is clear, Charles. I have no choice."

"If it was that clear, we wouldn't need a prefect of discipline."

"What are you suggesting?"

What Father Carmody was suggesting was that they put this little peccadillo in perspective. What was the big picture? Kincade was from Memphis, a son of the South; Notre Dame was a national university, but representation from the states of the old Confederacy was hardly what it should be. If Notre Dame got a reputation as hostile to the understandable pride of a noble if defeated enemy, the Mason-Dixon line would become the Berlin Wall.

He had gone on, even after he knew he had won the argument, caught up in the rhetoric of the case. Who cannot surprise in himself a sympathy for the Southern cause?

Before he got up to prepare for bed in a room that no longer had need of electric light, he thought of Quintin Kelly. Now in publishing, he had said. A nice fellow. But there was that look about him one sometimes saw on the faces of men waiting nervously in line to go to confession. Kelly was troubled in some way, and Father Carmody regretted that the circumstances had not been such that he might have gotten in a little pastoral work.

7　　　THE KINCADE TWINS, IDENTICAL

in size, weight, and even the cut of their red hair, had with admirable foresight arranged to meet with the Georgia Tech cheerleaders after the game and invited them for dinner.

"We can't go dressed like this," Babette Ashley squealed.

"More's the pity," Malcolm said. "How long will it take you to change?"

There were eight girls in the cheerleader squadron. It seemed excessive to invite them all, but the problem posed by cutting two from the herd was insurmountable. Besides, 8:2 odds had its attractions.

Babette was an old acquaintance if not friend of the twins, and the means of effecting the invitation.

"Where are the other boys?" the girls asked in chorus when seven of them along with Malcolm had been jammed into the back of the vehicle. Babette was up front with Eugene.

"Where do you think we're going?"

"I can't tell you two apart."

"Why should you?"

Malcolm had approved of Eugene's decision to scare up some other males. With just the two of them, this could become a farce. Finding a restaurant able to take them on such a day was of course out of the question. The solution was to repair to the dorm and have food brought in. Malcolm thoughtfully loaded several cases of contraband beer aboard so that the pizza and spaghetti did not go unaccompanied into the digestive systems of these increasingly jubilant young people. Additional males proved no problem, of course. Quite the opposite; now it was the girls who were the beneficiaries of favorable odds.

One might reasonably ask how the party would have developed had not one of the late invitees brought a copy of the current issue of the *Irish Rover*. Attention was drawn to the article on General Sherman and Notre Dame by Caleb Lanier.

"Let me see that," Malcolm demanded. He read in disbelief. Even if partially true, the burden of the story seemed a studied insult to the flowers of young Southern womanhood they were now plying with pasta and beer.

"We know him," Eugene said. "Football."

"A Yankee," Malcolm explained to their guests. But other copies of the offending issue had been brought, and the contents of the article were soon known to all.

"Notre Dame actually welcomed General Sherman here?" Babette spoke with indignation.

The eight Southern belles were profoundly offended. And what of themselves? Were they not compromised by fraternizing with the apparent enemy? What would Scarlett have said?

"We're as Southern as you are," Malcom insisted.

"At least," Eugene drawled.

"Then do something!" Babette demanded.

"But what?"

Babette didn't know. Neither did the other girls. Still, their demand seemed only reasonable. The question was how they could effectively demonstrate to these fine young women that they, had they been around at the time, would have protested the visit of the general whose scorched-earth policy as he marched to the sea was an ineradicable item in the annals of infamy.

"Is this a photograph of Sherman?" Babette asked, flourishing the paper.

"No, no. That's Father Corby."

"Who's Father Corby?"

A reasonable question, but it was met with silence. Then a reedy voice spoke up, that of a little nerd from North Dakota. He might have been reciting in class.

Father William Corby had applied to the governor of New York and been assigned as chaplain to the Irish Brigade under General Thomas Meagher. Corby was at the Battle of Fair Oaks, of Antietam, of Fredericksburg, Chancellorsville, the Wilderness, and Spotsylvania, sending the boys into battle with souls absolved of their sins. But it was at Gettysburg that the priest had risen to fame. The nerd from North Dakota indicated that the following passage in the article was taken from a history of Notre Dame written on the occasion of the centennial of the university by Father Arthur Hope.

The following morning the Irish Brigade was posted on Cemetery Ridge. In the valley below them was the little town. Just beyond the village, and only a mile away, the Confederates on Seminary Ridge could be clearly discerned. The battle began. The Third Corps was driven back by the Confederates. The Irish Brigade, until then held in reserve, must come to their assistance.

The reader stopped, as if for dramatic effect.

"Go on, go on."

At this juncture Father Corby approached Colonel Patrick Kelly, now in charge, saying to him: "For two or three weeks, we have been marching constantly. My men have not had a chance to get to confession. I must give them one last bit of spiritual comfort. Let me stand up on this rock, where they may all see me." It was so ordered. Above the terrible din of battle Father Corby told the men that since it was impossible at the moment to hear the confessions of the Catholic boys, they could be restored to the state of grace by prayerfully receiving the general absolution that he was about to impart. Let them, in their hearts, make a fervent act of contrition and a resolution to embrace the first opportunity of confession. As he finished these few words, and placed the purple stole over his shoulders, every man, Catholic and non-Catholic, fell to his knees. The chaplain's hand was raised in absolution.

"He's only blessing the Union army?" Babette addressed the question to Malcolm, for whom the information just given was as new as it was for her. "What about the Southern boys?"

"Corby's statue is in front of Corby Hall."

Malcolm looked at Eugene. Eugene looked at Malcolm. A family memory stirred. They put their red heads together, whispered briefly, then nodded in silent agreement.

A reconnaissance party was sent to Corby Hall and reported back that the feat proposed was impossible.

"You'd need a crane."

How does one thought produce another? Deep waters these, and not our present concern. In a trice, Malcolm was on the phone calling a nearby filling station. He had to call two others before he found one with a tow truck, and then he had to call a fourth to find one willing to send the vehicle to the Notre Dame campus.

Malcolm gave instructions on how to negotiate the gate. No guard would prevent a tow truck from coming to the aid of a campus motorist in distress.

"Who's in distress?"

"We need that truck."

The driver arrived in forty-five minutes. During the interval, more beer had strengthened the resolve of the gathering. For Malcolm and Eugene, what they proposed to do was a gallant gesture to their lovely guests, as well as a chance to trump their father's feat of long ago.

8　　THE HEADQUARTERS OF CAMPUS security represented a little island of peace on game days. Cars patrolled the campus, and many members of the force, on foot or bicycle, sauntered or wheeled among the partying fans, but there was really little to do save observe. The stadium was manned by an army of ushers, many of whom were the second or third generation of families who every game day donned an official-looking cap and took tickets at the gate or directed fans to their seats. The huge influx of traffic was the purview of the county sheriff and South Bend police, aided by another corps of volunteers who made sure that cars were parked in even rows and space maximally used. There was very little going on in headquarters, accordingly, and it was there with his iPod in his shirt pocket and plugs in his ears that Larry Douglas was ignoring his pudgy fiancée, Laura.

"Can you hear me when you're listening to that?"

Not to answer seemed a kind of lie, but Larry did not answer. He had downloaded some selections from Schopenhauer, misogynistic tidbits that were affording Larry culpable pleasure. His mother could not believe that he was engaged to Laura. Larry didn't quite believe it himself. Trying to reconstruct how the bargain had been entered into, he was sure that he had never proposed, not right out, anyway. It seemed that he had lost his freedom when he took advantage of Laura's amorous nature during long and sweaty sessions in his parked car.

"I wonder if I should go on working," Laura said. "After."

Had a solitary adverb ever sounded so ominous? "Why would you quit?" The thought that his paycheck would have to cover the two of them had not been among those weighing upon him. Until now. "What would you do all day?"

"What do other housewives do all day?"

"I don't know." His mother was a housewife, but she worked. He tried to think of a woman who just lolled around the house all day while her man was out working.

"I don't suppose there'd be just me for long." Her smile was meant to be seductive.

"What do you mean?"

She got up and came to him. "You know what I mean."

The phone rang, and Larry picked it up like a drowning man lunging for a life preserver. "Notre Dame Campus Security!"

He had to have the message repeated after he dug the plugs out of his ears.

"Some students stole my truck."

"Where are you calling from?"

"The front gate."

"Tell it to me in your own words."

"They stole my goddamn truck."

"I'll be right there." Larry was on his feet and halfway out the door when Laura screamed after him.

"Wait! I'll come with you."

"You're in charge here!"

He slammed the door and beat it out to his car.

When Larry went by the Grotto, he noticed some kind of commotion off to his left, no doubt a postgame celebration. At the guard shack, the driver glared at Larry.

"You security?"

"You the guy who lost his truck?"

This reminder of his humiliation softened the driver's attitude. "All I want is my truck back."

"You'll get your truck back. Don't worry about that."

The story was a simple one, but Larry wanted to hear it twice. He had never been in charge of an investigation before, or even of a complaint, and he was determined to do it by the book.

Jackson, the driver, had received a call about a car in distress behind the South Dining Hall. He got directions at the gate and drove to the dining hall, where a group of students awaited him.

"You sure they were students?"

"They sure looked like them."

"Lots of strangers on campus on a day like this."

The kids Jackson assumed were students had greeted him, talking all at once, explaining what the trouble was. Jackson got out of the truck and went around back to judge how best to hoist the car he was directed to. That's when his truck drove off.

"You'd left it running?"

"I just got out of the cab to see what the problem was."

"Why would anyone drive off in a tow truck?"

"You tell me. I went running after the truck like an idiot, and when I came back they were all gone. So, I walked back here and called you."

The first thing to do was to take Jackson back to headquarters. Larry wanted one more version of the story. He also wanted Laura to see him in operation. As he passed Old College, the commotion he had observed earlier was still going on in front of Corby Hall. He turned in.

"That's my truck," Jackson cried.

The truck in question had been backed across the lawn in front of Corby Hall. A chain from the raised derrick had been looped around the statue's shoulders. Even as Larry and Jackson watched, the truck began to move. It seemed to halt, then moved forward. Slowly the statue began to tip, and then, accompanied by a great roar from the onlookers, the effigy of the Rev. William Corby, CSC, third president of Notre Dame, Civil War chaplain, was ignominiously pulled from its base and toppled onto the lawn in front of the building named for him.

PART TWO

1 QUINTIN KELLY EMERGED FROM
drunken sleep smacking his lips,
unwilling to open his eyes, against the shut lids of which an
accusing unseen light was visible. First, a mental inventory.
Meditating monks had once begun their task by establishing
a sense of place; just so did Quintin strain to locate himself in
spatio-temporal coordinates. Shreds and fragments of memories raced across the bleak horizon of his mind. Magnus. He
opened his eyes and looked around.

The present bears a necessary relation to the past, but
memory is not always a reliable record of the link. He was on
a couch in an unfamiliar place. In blips and shards, an
episodic memory of the previous evening established itself in
his mind. He had managed to do what he had come to do,
speak with Magnus about Madeline, prepared for vilification,
anger, the righteousness of a man whose woman had done him
wrong. But what Quintin remembered was a bibulous camaraderie in which the two of them had seemed aligned against
the general dissolution of Western civilization. He had gained
the impression that Magnus had given him the go-ahead. Take
my wife, please.

This realization had been succeeded by euphoria. How different would his report of the conversation to Madeline be from what he had dreaded. And then, as if in proof that there are no depths that do not conceal a further subbasement of the soul, a horrible realization came. Madeline awaited word of his encounter with her husband. He brought his watch within a few inches of his eyes but could not discern the position of the hands upon its face. No matter. Whatever time it was was a time far beyond when he should have returned to the motel room where she was sitting alone awaiting news of their future, if any.

He swung his legs off the couch and levered himself to his feet. Immediately, he began to career across the room. In transit, he managed to aim himself toward a chair. He fell into it and it tipped backward, hung in the balance, and then slowly regained its original position. Quintin looked around. Magnus's apartment. It was hither they had come in the wee hours, long gone in alcoholic jubilation. Here they had sat for hours, exchanging remarks that failed to mesh but somehow amounted to communication, and then he had realized that Magnus was asleep in his chair. Quintin had a faint memory of deciding to rise and go. It might have been a moment before. First, he would shut his eyes and muster his forces. Between that moment and this stretched unconscious hours. Once more he brought his watch before his eyes. Nine thirty!

Slowly, carefully, he stood, his mind aroar with the lies he would tell Madeline to explain why he had let her spend an anxious night awaiting word that had not come. He found the bathroom, where he avoided his reflection in the mirror. He stooped over the basin and dashed water into his face. He lifted his head carefully and looked himself in the eyes. The sight was not as bad as he had feared. He washed his face and his domed bald head. He had to get to Madeline.

Call her. He extracted his cell phone and looked at it, as baffled as any member of a cargo cult when confronted with an artifact of an undreamt-of civilization. He did not know the number of the Tranquil Motel. For a frantic moment, he had wondered if he would even remember the name. He had to get there. So much was clear.

Back in the living room, shielding his eyes from the relentless daylight that poured in through the interstices between the slats in the window blinds, he listened. The stertorous complaint of snoring. He moved carefully in the direction of those primitive sounds. In a bedroom, Magnus lay diagonally across the bedspread like a bar sinister. Wake him? Why? The imperative was to get to Madeline. But how?

He returned to the living room. His eyes fell to the keys on the coffee table, and he had a vivid memory of Magnus tossing them there. He picked them up. He went to the door and let himself out.

He took the stairs to the ground level—four flights, but the thought of a descent in the elevator filled him with vertigo. He pushed down on the bar of a door and found himself outside, in a parking lot full of vehicles. Which was Magnus's? He looked at the keys and espied the plastic pod; he pressed UNLOCK and looked around him. On the third try, after moving about among the parked cars, he saw the winking lights he was looking for. A minute later he was headed out of the parking lot, bound for Madeline.

"Who is it?" a voice asked from behind the closed door he had refrained from opening with his plastic key.

"One or two," he had been asked when he registered, and he had answered as if he were confessing. Two. What in the world was the vision of the world that swarmed behind the bland expressions of such young people at motel reception desks?

"Quintin." He had brought his mouth against the panel of the door to speak his name. He repeated it, having moved back a bit, speaking more loudly.

Silence within. He had lifted his hand to knock when he heard a bolt being turned. The door opened, and Madeline looked at him over the protective chain. Had she locked him out or herself within? The expression on her face was unreadable.

"I'm back."

"Where have you been?"

"It's a long story."

She looked at him with amusement, as if from some vast height. The door closed, there was the sound of the chain, and then the door swung open.

"I've been with Magnus."

"Well, that must have been fun."

"Did you wait up for me?"

She smiled. "I met the most interesting people in the bar."

"Magnus isn't angry. Well, at first he was, then he settled down."

His story tumbled from his lips, disjointed, fragments of what he had said and what Magnus had said. While he spoke,

Madeline stood and began to fuss with a coffeepot, filling it with water, unwrapping a pod of coffee, pushing a button that made a light glow red. Was she listening?

"This is decaffeinated. That's all that's left. I already used the other."

"Forget the coffee!"

"You look awful."

"I feel awful."

"Take a shower. Shave."

He looked at her. Her expression varied between hauteur and amusement. She was treating him like a child. Like a drunk. He got to his feet and nearly lost his balance, as if to underscore her judgment of his condition. He lifted his unshaven chin and headed for the bathroom.

Under pelting water in the shower, his mind was filled with the present, a world of steam, of hot water, that seemed to release an overwhelming tiredness. How much had he slept? How little? He decided to postpone shaving. He got into bed naked, pulling the covers to his chin, and immediately sleep came.

2 WHEN THE DISHEVELED, BABBLING
Quintin finally returned to their motel,
Madeline had undergone a seismic change in her attitude
toward him. Anger that he had not even bothered to telephone,
let alone that he had come back at an indecent hour? Not at
all. She listened almost clinically—better, artistically—to his
explanation of where he had spent the night. It was incredible
to her that she had ever regarded this pathetic person as her
mentor, had ever encouraged him to think that if she were free
of Magnus . . . She shuddered at the suggestion. Her entire
world had turned over since her meeting with Rufus James
the night before.

Magnus mocked her writing, of course, but then he was
jealous, as she had not been loath to tell him.

"Jealous of that schlock!" He actually threw a copy of *Maid
in Vicksburg* across the room. It bounced on a sofa cushion
and fell to the floor, opening its pages as if to cushion the fall.
"Oh, sure. I wish I could write immortal accounts of games no
one will remember tomorrow.'

He had a point, of course, and one she was perfectly capa-
ble of making to herself. As a girl Madeline had written poetry;
in college she had tried her hand at short stories, but she

hadn't even made it into campus publications. Unfed, unencouraged, her ambition grew. She was an avid reader of book jackets; she collected literary gossip; she felt she was part of a sorority whose password had not been given to her. She joined a writers' club and was almost shocked at the commercial ambitions of the others. What they wanted was sales, money, big money. It occurred to Madeline that she had never looked on writing in that way. To write was to convey some sliver of her soul to a worthy reader she did not know. The vulgarity of the club had its attractions, though. She told herself that she could turn out the kind of thing the others longed to write. And she could. She sat down at her computer and accepted her own dare, and the odd thing was that all the solemn seriousness with which she had always written fled. This was a game. It was a game she learned to play to a fare-thee-well.

The day before yesterday, even yesterday, early, she would have attributed her success to Quintin. He had responded to her first submission with a lengthy and helpful letter. They became pen pals, collaborators of a sort. He seemed more interested in her becoming a published author than she was. Never spoken between them, but understood, was the fact that the kind of fiction she was writing was, well, schlock. But there was all that money, and fame of a sort, anonymous fame. There were still times when she managed to think of herself as Margaret Mitchell, embarked on a novel that would be both a commercial and critical success. That never happened. She was a heroine at her writers' club before she drifted away.

Magnus had approved. "Never play golf with someone with a high handicap," he advised. "You will sink to the level of the competition." He spoke with authority, and no wonder; the mantel was cluttered with the trophy cups and plaques he brought home. But it wasn't her skill that was in question, only the league she had joined. They were alike, she and Magnus; he was a good amateur, but his game would never gain him admission to the ranks of professionals. What her success entailed was the affair with Quintin; it might have been his fee.

When Magnus's silly book came out and he was scheduled to sign copies at the Notre Dame bookstore, this suggested a neutral site where Quintin could inform Magnus of their plans.

While Quentin went to the game, she watched it for a time on the television in the room but became bored and sought out the motel bar. The game was on, of course, and stools along the bar were filled with noisy fans. She wandered to a table in a corner, far from the madding crowd. As she sipped her drink, she realized that eyes were on her. Honestly. He sat alone at a table, ignoring the game, staring at her. What on earth was the matter with him? Then his face became familiar—but it couldn't be.

He picked up his drink and joined her. "Don't I know you?"

She laughed. "I had just been thinking I recognized you."

"Rufus James."

She actually squealed. "I knew it. What in heaven's name are you doing here?"

Of course she knew all about him. He lived in Memphis; he

wrote savage dismissals of fiction for the *New York Review of Books*; he had published one novel that earned him comparison with Faulkner and Tate. She had pored over his entry in the *Dictionary of Literary Biography*. She leaned toward him. "I loved *Dixie Coup*. I love it more every time I read it."

"Ah, one of my handful of readers."

"What are you writing now?"

He scowled and looked away. "Never ask a writer what he's writing."

"I'm sorry."

His scowl went away. "It's only a venial sin." He sipped his drink. "I talk like that whenever I come back to Notre Dame."

He was an alumnus, she knew that; she knew all about him. Magnus had no memory of ever having heard of Rufus James, although their times on campus had overlapped.

He finished his drink; she finished hers; they had another. All she wanted was for him to talk, and he talked. He confided that he had come to South Bend in order to stir up memories for something he was writing. "I didn't know there was a home game this weekend. I was lucky to get a room."

"Here?"

"Ha. North of Niles."

"So you are writing another novel."

"That's twice. Now it's a mortal sin." He lifted his glass in a toast. "Yes, I am writing another novel. I've been writing the damned thing for six years."

Writer's block? She had heard of it but never experienced it.

"You've read only *Dixie Coup*?"

She was puzzled.

"You wouldn't know my other novels."

She looked over his head.

"I'm a writer, too."

He hunched over the table, combing his beard with his fingers. There were pouches under his eyes and permanent lines on his forehead. He wore his hair long, and it was shot with gray. Everything about him spelled Author. "Tell me."

She fished *Dancing in Charleston* from her purse and put it on the table. He picked it up almost reverently, turning it in his hand, riffling the pages, looking at her. His eyes met hers, then drifted away. He finished his drink and rattled the ice in the glass, about to take a gamble.

"I'll tell you a secret."

His secret was that he wrote thrillers under a pseudonym. "Blood and guts, ripped bodices, the whole thing."

"I don't believe it! How many?"

He ticked them off on his fingers. None of the titles meant anything to her. He patted *Dancing in Charleston*.

"A couple of hacks," he murmured.

"Don't say that about yourself."

"How many of these have you written?"

She told him. He seemed impressed. Madeline was confused. Rufus James was everything she once had dreamed of becoming. A writer of renown. His merciless put-down of Updike was quoted at cocktail parties from coast to coast. His novel had been praised to the skies. Was it known that he published thrillers?

"My reputation is in your hands. I don't know why I told you."

Madeline thought she knew. It was meant to be. He was a great writer who was spoiling his talent writing thrillers. He needed someone to steer him back onto the right track, someone to cherish and nurture his talent.

"I never heard of Juniper Press," he said, looking at her novel.

"They're in Athens, Georgia."

"Good Lord."

"They've been very good to me."

"I would say you've been very good to them. Look, if you're going to write this kind of fiction, you should make as much from it as you can. What other satisfaction is there?"

If Magnus had said such a thing she would have hit him. But this was Rufus James.

"You need a New York publisher. A mainline publisher."

"Who?"

"Mine."

"You mean it?"

"You want to switch, say the word. My recommendation would be enough."

"How much more?"

He looked at her. He looked at her novel. "You want to tell me what you make on one of these?"

She said it in whispers. To her, it was a princely sum.

He shook his head. "You could triple that. Quadruple that. Your books would be in every airport in the nation. That's where books are sold. Do you know how many flights in and out of this country's airports there are every day? Bored travelers, most of them women, they'd snap up something like this."

"I'm in your hands." A fleeting image of Quintin came and went, but he had joined the ranks of the discarded.

How many drinks did they have? The game seemed to have ended; more people came into the bar. They had to sit closer and closer in order to hear one another.

A large figure loomed over their table. "Madeline O'Toole?"

A grinning boy, good-looking, red hair. Perhaps elsewhere she would have known immediately who he was.

"Eugene Kincade." His smile broadened. He had yet to look at Rufus James.

"Did he say O'Toole?"

"Madeline Butler's a pen name."

The Kincade boy had drawn up a chair and joined them. "We're from Memphis," he explained to James.

"There was an O'Toole here when I was," James said. "He was signing books in the bookstore earlier."

Eugene Kincade was a lovely boy, and in other circumstances she would have been delighted to run into him, but this was not that occasion. She had been deep in conversation with a legendary writer who was confiding in her as if he, too, realized there was something predestined about their meeting. James had pushed back from the table, clearly irked that they had been interrupted.

"Eugene," Madeline said, laying a hand on his arm as she, too, pushed back from the table. "We were just leaving."

"You can't leave now."

Can and did. Madeline felt rude in just leaving Eugene like that, but what could she do. She had to continue her fascinating conversation with Rufus James.

She led him out of the bar and along the corridor to her room.

Two hours later she was feeling like a tramp in one of her novels. No, that wasn't true. This was different. She lay on the bed—James was in the bathroom—scarcely believing what had happened. Of course she had drunk too much. Again she thrust away a thought that sat in judgment on the incredibly passionate scene she had just enacted with the ardent Rufus James. A knock on the door lifted her from the bed. She wrapped a blanket around herself. James looked out from the bathroom fresh from the shower. His hair and beard gave him the appearance of a wet mop. She put a finger to her lips and shook her head. She didn't know what lie she would tell Quintin, but she would not let him in.

When she eased the door open, she looked out over the chain at Eugene Kincade.

"I got your room number from the desk," he said in loud slurred tones. "I came to apologize."

"You have no reason to apologize."

"I made a damned pest of myself, and I'm sorry."

There were others behind him now, people peeking out of their doors, curious or angry at this noisy exchange.

"Eugene, go away."

"Damn it, I came to apologize and I'm going to."

She shut the door. He began pounding on it, proclaiming his intention to make a proper apology. Good Lord.

Rufus James came into the room, dressed, bright as a penny. "What's going on?"

She tried to explain, trying to laugh as she did so.

"I'll get rid of him," James said.

He unchained the door and stepped outside. She heard them talking, and then the voices went away.

Rufus James did not return. It was for him that she had sat waiting, not Quintin.

3 FOR THE SECOND TIME THAT DAY
Quintin Kelly awoke in confusion, but
this time he was sober. He lay looking at the stippled ceiling
of the motel bedroom trying to reconstruct what he had said to
Madeline when he returned. He turned on his side and saw a
ring of keys on the table beside him. Car keys. Slowly the
memory of driving off in Magnus's rental car came to him.
What a rotten trick to pull: first his wife, then his rental car.

There were voices in the other room. He sat up and listened, Madeline and a male voice. Southern, very Southern.
That was the drawl that Magnus had not mastered. When he
went, dressed and presentable, into the other room, a very tall
red-haired young man rose and stared at him.

"Quintin Kelly," he said, going toward the young man with
his hand out. The boy backed away.

"This is Eugene Kincade," Madeline said in an odd voice.
"From Memphis."

The young man was clearly shocked at the sight of the
strange man who had emerged from Mrs. O'Toole's bedroom.

"Eugene came to take me to the noon Mass at Sacred
Heart."

Good Lord, it was Sunday. He had forgotten Madeline was

Catholic. It was a long time since he himself had practiced the faith of his fathers.

"Go ahead," Quintin said. "I have to get Magnus's car back to him."

"His car?"

Quintin spoke to the boy. "I brought the O'Toole car here a little while ago."

The boy's expression altered. Belatedly he took Quintin's hand. Quintin felt that he had just rescued Madeline's reputation.

"I made a fool of myself last night," Eugene said.

"Just give me a minute," Madeline said hurriedly. She dashed into the bedroom.

"I made a pest of myself last night," Eugene explained to Quentin. "In the bar. I came back to apologize, and Rufus James led me away. Thank God."

"Rufus James?"

"They were together in the bar. I just burst in on them, and they came back here—" He paused. His thoughts moved visibly across his bright innocent face. Madeline and Rufus James. Madeline and Quintin Kelly. He was clearly confused, and shocked. Madeline came out of the bedroom.

Quintin said, "We've been talking about Rufus James."

"Isn't that amazing? I went out to the bar—for the game—and ran into him."

"I didn't know you knew him."

"I don't! I didn't. We just met."

If Eugene's face was a mask of innocence, Madeline's read like a police blotter. Quintin recalled her odd reaction when at last he had returned. The boy said Madeline had brought James to the room.

"You'd better hurry if you're going to make the noon Mass."

"Are you coming?"

"First I have to return Magnus's car."

Madeline put her arm through Eugene's. Quintin opened the door and saw them out. After he had shut it on them, he stood for a moment looking at the rectangle of door. After several minutes, he opened it again and went out to Magnus's car.

4   ➤ THE VIBRATION OF THE CELL phone in his shirt pocket wakened Magnus O'Toole. He got it out and opened it.

"Magnus." His voice seemed to come from far away. He repeated his name after he had opened his eyes. It still sounded odd.

"You're fired!"

"Who is this?" Of course it was Barker in Atlanta. Barker fired people on an average of once a week. Theatrics, of course. The union would have his scalp, if he had one, for such autocratic behavior.

"I ran a wire service story. You can sell yours to the athletic department there. If I want a press release from Notre Dame I can get it for nothing."

"How's everything else?"

"Do you know how little space you devoted to Georgia Tech?"

"It wasn't much of a game."

"Who would know that from what you sent in? You even misspelled the name of the Georgia Tech quarterback."

"That's the checker's fault."

"And trying to push your book in an account of a game!"

"I sold hundreds."

"Then you'll have something to live on."

"Am I still fired?"

"Not until you get back here and I can do it face-to-face."

"Thanks for calling."

The line went dead. Magnus studied his cell phone, imagining a satellite in outer space relaying earthly voices to one another. All that technology, and for what? So Barker could try to ruin his day.

He turned on the television and saw a table full of imbeciles talking politics. Sunday morning. Well, Sunday anyway. He turned off the set. His head was light and his stomach was empty. He went barefoot to the kitchen and found a box of cereal, but the milk in the refrigerator looked months old. He decided not to risk it. A bowl of dry cereal is not a good way to address one's hunger. He found some juice and tasted it. It seemed to have fermented. And then he thought of poor Quintin Kelly. Had Quintin actually made a declaration of love for Madeline?

"Quintin!"

He seemed to have gone. Magnus checked the other bedroom, and it was empty. The living room was a mess. He frowned at the glasses and checked the bottle on the coffee table to see if it was empty. It was. A good thing. Better to drink fermented fruit juice than to start the day with a drink.

Sunday. A residual conscience began to remind him how far he had drifted from the practices of his youth. He should get to Mass. He should go to confession. A clean slate, that's what he needed, a new Magnus about to embark on life without Madeline. He could get an annulment. That would be like the negation of a negation. What kind of a marriage did they have? He had wanted children, and all she wanted was a career writing dirty books. No marriage court in the country would refuse him. Besides, she had apparently been playing around with Quintin Kelly. By contrast, Magnus felt pure as the driven snow. So he drank too much. He could always quit. He often did. And don't forget *Irish Icons*. The book seemed a first step in the new life he meant to lead.

He sat down to think of it and then wished he hadn't. The thought of having to get to his feet again was daunting. But why should he stand up? Better to sit here and think of the new life he longed to live. He was still sitting there when Quintin came back.

"I returned your car."

"What car?"

"The rental." Quintin tossed the keys on the coffee table. The jangling noise seemed to reverberate through Magnus's head.

"I saw Madeline."

"She's in Memphis."

"I told you last night. We came up together. To give you the bad news."

"All I heard was good news. I wish you joy."

"Go to hell."

"I'm missing Mass."

"So am I. Madeline went with one of her admirers."

"To Mass?"

"A student from Memphis. A redhead. Apparently Rufus James took off."

"You're not making a lot of sense."

It didn't make much more sense when Quintin tried to make a coherent tale of it. He had gone back to Madeline like a whipped cur, expecting to catch hell for staying out all night, and she had brushed it off as if it didn't matter. "Not that she was lonely. How long has she known Rufus James?"

"I didn't know she did. Who is he?"

"The author."

"Never heard of him."

"He's the kind of author Madeline would like to be."

"I'm an author."

"He's the other kind."

"Well, Madeline's not."

"You're damned right she isn't." Quintin's eyes were moist. "I molded that woman, Magnus. I practically wrote her first book for her."

"God is merciful."

"Well, I'm not. The woman has the attention span of a fruit fly."

"Don't they die when they mate?"

"I'm not a voyeur." There were actual tears leaking from Quintin's eyes. "The hell with her."

"I thought you were in love with her."

"Oh, shut up."

Quintin picked up the remote and got a local station, where they followed the news of the statue being pulled down on campus.

"Father Corby!" Magnus cried. "That's a sacrilege. What kind of fans does Georgia Tech have?"

"Listen. They say it was Notre Dame students."

"The place is going to hell."

There was footage of the fallen Corby. A tow truck was parked on the lawn. Then the man who owned the truck was interviewed. He told his story with a mixture of anger and shame. The reporter asked how anyone could just steal his truck.

Jackson glared at her. "You ever have a truck stolen?"

"No."

"Neither did I, before this."

It seemed a small claim to fame. The prefect of discipline was interviewed and said that everything was under control. The students responsible would face severe discipline. Then a student appeared on the screen.

"I did it," he said, looking into the camera, chin up, his red hair tousled. "No one else is responsible. I'll take whatever punishment they hand out."

"Why did you do it?"

"I'm from Memphis."

"That's him!" Quintin said, going to the set for a closer look. "That's the student who took Madeline to Mass."

His name was Kincade, and he tried to tell a story about his father, but the interview was cut off.

"That must have been on tape. That boy and Madeline should still be at Mass."

5 ROGER KNIGHT DROVE HIS GOLF
cart to Sacred Heart Basilica for Mass
and afterward was drawn to the scene on the front lawn of
Corby. Yellow tape fluttered in the breeze, marking off the
scene. Television crews jostled one another. The commanding
figure of Father Corby lay on its side on the grass. In the cold
light of day, what must have seemed an innocent prank took
on the dimensions of an assault on the tradition of Notre
Dame.

When Roger got back to the apartment, Father Carmody
was there.

"I wonder if anyone knows who Corby was," the old priest
grumbled. "Next I suppose they'll pull down a statue of Our
Lord."

"Remember the Visitation," Roger murmured.

The magnificent statue of Elizabeth greeting Mary fash-
ioned by Father Lauck stands in front of the bookstore. It had
hardly been put in place when it was desecrated.

Father Carmody nodded. "Not inadvertent."

"I have been speaking of Father Corby in my course on
Notre Dame and the Civil War."

"Perhaps we ought to go down your class list to find the culprits."

"They aren't known?"

Father Carmody winced. "I don't understand the younger generation. All they had to do was lie low. The thing would have blown over . . ." His eyes widened. "Thank God no one can hear me mouthing such heresy."

Phil said, "Perhaps that's what they will do."

"Not at all, not at all. We have a public confession of guilt."

"Good heavens. Who is it?"

"Malcolm Kincade." Father Carmody chuckled. "Maybe I do understand the younger generation. This is a boy intent on doing his father one better."

And Father Carmody told the Knights of the effort of Kincade père many years ago.

"I played a small role in preventing his expulsion from the university. I wonder if I can do the same for the son."

"But why the family animus against Father Corby?"

"The family is from Memphis."

"Ah."

"I don't get it," Phil said.

"Notre Dame was all but identified with the Union side in the Civil War, Phil. Priests served as chaplains, nuns worked in hospitals. Corby was merely the most prominent among them. Because of Gettysburg."

"Roger, the Civil War ended a century and a half ago."

"So the books tell us."

It was young Kincade's confession—to the local media, not to the prefect of discipline—that had brought Father Carmody to them this morning. The postgame prank had been covered in the national media, and there had been a spot on ESPN by their resident critic of all things Irish, in all cases with a lighthearted touch. Father Carmody was intent that the incident fade gently away lest it be turned into a criticism of Notre Dame. Both Roger and Phil had been struck on other occasions by Father Carmody's intense concern for the reputation of the university. Despite a long lifetime of experience of undergraduates, the priest seemed to regard his knowledge of them as something of a trade secret, not to be divulged to those beyond the campus—unless, of course, they were alumni, and even for them facts had to be buffed and shined a bit before export. Father Carmody's role as guardian angel of Notre Dame had in the past been a legitimate extension of his job description, but what is the job description of an éminence grise? Father Carmody had been that éminence long before his silver shock of hair settled him completely in the role.

"So what will you do, Father?"

Before the question could be answered, the doorbell rang. Phil answered it and admitted Caleb Lanier.

He came forward three steps, stopped, and looked around abjectly. "It's all my fault."

"That is a very comprehensive confession," Father Carmody said.

"It was my article on Father Corby that set them off. Their sister is . . ." He hesitated. "A good friend of mine. She told me all about it."

Only in fiction is information doled out to the reader in

coherent and sequential form. Caleb obeyed the looser laws of ordinary communication, and it was some time before the Knight brothers and Father Carmody understood.

"The South will rise again," Roger murmured.

"And Father Corby must fall," said Father Carmody.

Over the next half hour, a strategy was planned. Father Carmody and Phil would seek out the Kincade brothers and put out the fire.

"It was General Sherman that did it." Caleb meant that the Kincade brothers had been incensed to learn that Notre Dame had been host to General Sherman's family during the Civil War and, when the fighting was over, feted and honored him on campus.

A tempest in a teapot? Indeed, indeed. But the following day a far more serious problem fell on the shoulders of Father Carmody and the Knight brothers.

6   MARIA CONCEPCIÓN HAD JOINED
the great northward migration five years
ago and ended up in this state a portion of whose border
hugged Lake Michigan. Moving through states with names
that made them seem an extension of her homeland—
Arizona, Texas—and others whose names seemed arguably
Spanish—Oklahoma, Nebraska—she had ended here in Indiana. Summers were agreeably hot if not so agreeably humid,
but with fall came the chill that would turn to bitter cold and
bring doubts about the wisdom of her move. In the Tranquil
Motel, where she worked, she was surrounded by others with
similar backgrounds; the conversations in the corridors as
rooms were cleaned and readied for new occupants were all in
Spanish. Sometimes Maria Concepción imagined that she was
home and the people who came and went were tourists from
elsewhere.

The task of the housekeeper was complicated by the fact
that guests left throughout the morning. On the corridor
assigned to her and Rosita, they moved like checkers from
emptied room to emptied room, coming back to those whose
occupants remained almost to the noon checkout time. That
Monday, twelve o'clock came and went, and still there was no

answer to their knock on the door of room 320. Rosita grew impatient. She wanted a smoke. Maria Concepción told her to go outside and have her cigarette. Meanwhile, she called the desk and was assured again that the guests in 320 were scheduled to leave that day.

"Two?"

"Two. Mr. and Mrs. Kelly."

"They don't answer my knock."

Was it possible that they had already left and this delay was pointless? Maria Concepción became as impatient as Rosita had been. She marched down to 320, unlocked the door, pushed it ajar, and called, "Housekeeper."

She cocked her head, but there was no answer. She pushed her way into the suite.

"Housekeeper."

She kept saying that as she moved around the sitting room. The bedroom door was closed. Maria tapped on it, calling out. She waited, listening, but there was no sound from the other side of the door. Should she open the bedroom door as she had opened the door to the hall? She wished Rosita would get back. You could count on Rosita to do the daring thing. Maria's hand closed on the knob of the door. She turned it and pushed.

"Housekeeper."

There was a sound behind her, and she turned. She breathed again. It was Rosita.

"What's going on?"

"I think they must have left already."

Rosita brushed past her and sauntered into the room as if

she were the manager. Maria was about to follow when Rosita screamed.

She rushed out of the bedroom, still screaming, her eyes wide with fright.

If Rosita had daring, Maria Concepción had calmness. She leaned into the bedroom and looked around.

The woman lay on the bed, more undressed than dressed, and she stared at Maria with wide unblinking eyes, the eyes of the dead.

1

MIKE BEATTY, THE TRANQUIL Motel manager, gave the excited jabber of the cleaning women only half an ear, but he heard them. A dead body in 302, *nombre de Cristo*! But it was important to him to retain the hierarchical gap between himself and Maria Concepción and Rosita and all the rest of them who reminded him of how far he himself had come, and how easily he could be tugged back down to their status. Of course, new employees couldn't put together his name and the fact that he looked like one of them. He had picked up the name when going through Texas.

"Excuse me?" he said to Rosita.

She repeated the message in English.

"How do you know she's dead?"

"How do I know you're a dumb sonofabitch?" She said that in Spanish, which Beatty pretended not to understand.

He fluttered a ringed hand at the women. "I'll check it out in a minute."

They withdrew across the lobby, whispering fiercely to one another. Rosita went right on outside and lit a cigarette. Beatty was aware of her glaring eyes upon him as he feigned work at the counter. It was in such small ways that one established and then retained authority. Then he went down the hall to Kitty Callendar's office. Kitty, the bookkeeper, had in her own mind fallen on evil days and regarded the Tranquil Motel as little better than a brothel. She took obvious delight when they raised the rates during Notre Dame home game weekends. She could hear the raucous celebrating in the bar and restaurant; she was kept informed by the housekeepers of what went on in the rooms.

"You speak Spanish?" Michael had asked her.

Kitty Callendar opened a gap between thumb and forefinger.

Now she swung away from her computer when he entered her office, her brows lifting imperiously. She wore her dyed hair in a kind of bird's nest atop her narrow head, which seemed put on display by the scrawny neck that emerged from her fluffy blouse.

"What is it, Miguel?"

He ignored that. His secret was their little secret, that's what calling him Miguel implied.

"There's a dead body in 302."

"My God." But her eyes lit up as if all her theories of the motel were suddenly realized.

"At least that's what the housekeepers say. Of course they're hysterical. I want you to come with me while I check it out."

"Me?" Her facade cracked and threatened to crumble, but then she straightened her bony shoulders and stood. The gleam was back in her eyes.

He led the way down the long corridor, the muffled clump

of Kitty's heels assuring him that she was following. He held the master key before him as if they were engaged in some sort of ceremonial procession. Before turning the corner, he looked back. Kitty's expression was one of eager dread. Maria Concepción was watching them from a distance. Michael made an ambiguous gesture in her direction and then resumed the march to 302.

The door was wide open. He put the master key in his pocket and put his head inside the door.

"Manager."

Kitty went past him into the suite and stood in the middle of the sitting room, looking about her with disgust. The glasses and bottles and overflowing ashtray spelled mindless riot to her, and she was pleased.

Michael went on into the bedroom and immediately withdrew. "There is a body." He was so shaken he spoke Spanish.

Kitty went in and stood beside the bed, looking at the woman sprawled there. She took a corner of the bedspread and pulled it over the body.

"Is she dead?"

"Of course she's dead."

"I'll call a doctor."

She made a face. "Call the police."

He picked up the phone beside the bed, trying to ignore the sightless eyes of the dead woman. He could remember when she checked in, the Kellys, Mr. and Mrs. Where was Mr. Kelly? Several other guests had called the desk to complain about 302. He put down the phone before dialing and crossed to the bathroom, half expecting to find another body in there.

The place was a mess, towels hanging everywhere, a night-gown on the hook behind the door, cosmetics and all the mysterious contents of a woman's purse scattered about the marble surface in which the basin was sunk. With an unsteady hand he pulled back the shower curtain and felt a flood of relief to find the shower unoccupied. He went back into the bedroom. Kitty was staring down at the dead woman like the angel of judgment.

Michael Beatty picked up the phone again and dialed 302. What was he doing? He depressed the cradle and hit 9 and then 911.

2

JIMMY STEWART OF SOUTH BEND homicide was notified of the dead body found in the Tranquil Motel out on 31 and suggested they let Roseland know. Roseland commanded several miles of the highway and supported itself on traffic tickets issued with the random selectivity of the state lottery.

"They don't do homicide."

"How do you know it's homicide?" Jimmy asked.

"That's what you're going to find out."

He hung up, hungover. He had watched the Notre Dame game Saturday in a sports bar and stayed on, closing the place. When he got back to his apartment, he had what he called a nightcap but what might have been a ten-gallon Stetson. On Sunday, he had caught the noon Mass on television and spent the rest of the day watching pro games and sipping restorative cans of light beer. Sunday night he drove to a roadhouse just across the Michigan state line and had a huge hamburger with raw onions and more beer. Half a dozen television sets plus a huge screen brought in more football. He could learn to hate football. When he drove home, aiming his headlights through a softly falling rain, he had been filled with self-pity. There were times when he actually missed his wife, who had called it quits a couple of years ago and flown to Vegas, where she ran up a huge number on a credit card before he canceled it. She was now living with her sister in Encino.

Now, on Monday morning, it occurred to him that he must have driven past the motel where the body of a woman had been reported. After a cup of coffee and a tasteless Pop-Tart, he headed for the Tranquil Motel.

The woman was definitely dead. He called downtown to summon the medical examiner and sealed off the room. Then he talked to employees.

"You the manager?" he asked the stick figure with the funny hairdo.

She told him coldly that she was Kitty Callendar, the book-keeper. Kitty. The name suggested someone warm and cuddly. The name didn't fit her. Neither did the name Michael Beatty fit the manager.

"She check in alone?"

"No. With her husband."

"Where's he?"

"I don't know."

Jimmy looked at the credit card record that had been made when the couple checked in.

"There were complaints about her," Kitty said, her eyebrows lifting significantly.

"What kind of complaints?"

"Other guests. There was a lot of traffic to 302. Arguments in the hallway."

"Between the Kellys?"

"Not just them."

"They had visitors?"

"I'm only telling you what I heard. From guests who complained."

"They complained about noise on a football weekend?"

Jankowski, the medical examiner, arrived, along with the crew from the lab to take prints and photos of the scene. Jimmy gave them half an hour and then went to 302.

Jankowski rubbed his nose with the back of his hand. He still wore rubber gloves. "No marks on the body."

"She was only half dressed."

"Asphyxiation. That's my present guess."

"Smothered?"

Jankowski grew cautious. "I'll be in a better position to say when I've taken her in."

Jimmy took another look at the body. A good-looking woman, for whatever good it did her now. He checked with the lab crew.

"Any signs of a male occupant?"

"Like what?"

"She checked in with a husband."

There were two razors in the bathroom, one a man's. Jimmy watched them bag it, wondering if they were sealing the fate of the absent Mr. Kelly along with his razor. He went into the lobby to get a phone number for the address on the credit card. Athens, Georgia. He told the operator to dial the number.

"Did you write it down?"

He rattled the number back to her. From far off in Athens,

Georgia, he got a busy signal. Jankowski was passing through the lobby, and Jimmy hailed him. The body had been taken out through a service entrance in back.

"Check for sexual activity."

Jankowski just looked at him. "I'll check for everything."

"Just telling you how to do your job."

"How's yours going?"

"Nowhere."

In the bar a chubby little waitress with PHYLLIS on her name tag brought him a beer.

"You work on Saturday?"

She looked at him as if this were an overture. "Which Saturday?" A cute smile.

"Last Saturday."

"Don't talk to me about last Saturday." She looked around the room as if visions of Saturday's customers were forming in her memory.

"Tell me about it."

Phyllis told him about it. Every table taken, people standing, which was against the law, except at the bar, but this was football Saturday so anything went.

"So what? Half the employees are illegals."

"Underage?"

Nice laugh to go with the smile. She explained. Phyllis was all for building a mile-high fence along the Mexican border. All the cleaning staff were immigrants, as well as the busboys.

"Did you talk with Green Card at the desk?"

"Beatty?"

"You think that's his real name?"

"You don't."

"Take a good look at him."

She was probably right. But as Phyllis said, so what? It's a nation of immigrants.

"We found a dead body in 302."

"Come on."

"What do you think I'm doing here?"

She stepped back and squinted at him. "You a cop?"

"Detective Jimmy Stewart."

"You mean that about a dead body?"

"A woman named Kelly." He described her.

Phyllis's eyes lifted. "The Southern belle? She watched the game in here. Picked up some guy, and then they went off together."

"To her room?"

"How would I know a thing like that?"

"I just want an educated guess."

"It was a football Saturday."

"If it comes to that, could you recognize him again?"

"Now just a minute. I don't want to get involved."

"We hardly know one another."

A nice intimate chortling laugh. Her name should be Kitty. He asked her about the bookkeeper.

"She never drinks in here."

"She looks like a teetotaler."

"Ha. Green Card brings her a manhattan after lunch and another before she goes home. He sits with her while she drinks it."

"You can see all that from here?"

"Rosita told me. I got curious as to where the manhattans were going. Green Card doesn't drink. He gets mad when I offer him tequila."

"Give me another of these."

He used the bar phone to call the number in Athens, Georgia, again, and this time he got an answer.

"Juniper Press."

Jimmy was surprised. "Mr. Kelly, please."

"Mr. Kelly is out of town."

"South Bend?"

"How did you know that?"

He identified himself.

"Has something happened to Mr. Kelly?"

"Do you have a number for Mrs. Kelly?"

"Mrs. Kelly? There's no Mrs. Kelly." The woman sounded indignant.

Jimmy thanked her.

"But you have to tell me. Is something wrong?"

"I'll be in touch. Tell Mr. Kelly I called."

"Then he's all right."

"As far as I know."

Phyllis had moved down the bar while he made his call and was leafing through the paper. She let out a little cry and hurried to Jimmy, turning the page so he could see it.

"What am I looking for?"

It was a story about a statue that had been pulled down on the Notre Dame campus, with a photograph of a student who was responsible.

"He was in here Saturday night."

"You remember all the boys?"

"This one I do. Isn't he good-looking?"

"It says he was pulling down a statue on the Notre Dame campus Saturday night."

"He was here. How could I forget a face like that?"

"You're making me jealous."

"Oh, he was just a kid."

"I used to be a kid."

"So was I."

The student's name was Malcolm Kincade, and he was from Memphis. Pulling down a statue seemed a strange way to celebrate a victory.

Downtown, Jimmy checked out the dead woman's purse and found out that her name was not Kelly but O'Toole. Madeline O'Toole from Atlanta. She seemed to own a condo in Memphis as well. There was a paperback novel in the purse, too. *Dancing in Charleston* by Madeline Butler. Jimmy wondered if there was a Mr. O'Toole. This Kincade boy seemed to be the only way he was going to find someone who had talked to the dead woman.

3 THE SHOCKING NEWS THAT THE statue of the third president of Notre Dame had been toppled from his pedestal on Saturday night provided a welcome topic of conversation at the Old Bastards' table in the University Club at the group's Monday lunch.

Armitage Shanks addressed his fellow emeriti with mock solemnity. "This may be only the beginning, gentlemen."

"Iconoclasm," said Bingham, once professor of law and now dispenser of free and irrelevant legal advice to the group.

"There was a man on campus Saturday selling a book about Notre Dame icons."

"Is he in favor of clasm?"

"His name is O'Toole."

"Not O'Clasm?"

"Why would they topple Corby's statue?" Potts asked.

"Do you remember him?"

"He was already in bronze when I joined the faculty."

"Ah, the bronze age."

"It is the destiny of presidents nowadays. Look at Ted and Ned."

"Where?"

"In front of the library."

"They put Moose Krause on a bench."

"Don't forget Leahy."

"And Saddam Hussein."

"Was he a coach?"

"A president. They pulled down his statue."

"I don't remember him."

Debbie, the hostess, brought a copy of the *Observer* to the table and showed them the photograph of the student who claimed responsibility for bringing Father Corby to earth as a protest against the university's siding with the North in the Civil War. "Is it true?"

"What?"

"Did we take sides?"

"Ask Potts. He was a drummer boy."

Horvath, who had taught history, began a lecture on Notre Dame's involvement in the War Between the States, but he was ignored, as he had been by generations of students.

"Who was General Sherman?" Debbie asked.

"Tanks."

"You're welcome."

The administration, doubtless fearing a precedent, had decided to make an event of replacing the statue on its pedestal.

"You would think a chapel had been desecrated," Shanks said. "Is there a special blessing for past presidents?"

"Where are statues of the faculty?" Potts asked querulously.

"Hold that pose."

"Potts in bronze."

"I'll drink to that."

Debbie summoned the waitress. "Another round."

The OBs unwisely drank at lunch, the caution of their active years long forgotten. Now that smoking was banned in the club, a noontime drink was their only means of showing their scorn for the health nuts of the day.

Bingham, who drank mineral water, asked if they objected to wellness.

"I always object when adverbs are turned into substantives."

"Have you stopped running?"

"Only at the nose."

"His name is Kincade," Debbie said, referring to the story in the *Observer*. "A nice-looking boy."

"That is how serial murderers are usually described by neighbors."

"Oh, come on. It was just a prank."

"He was with the troops at Gettysburg," Horvath said.

"That is what his statue commemorates. It was only later that he became president."

"Of the North or South?"

Potts had removed his hearing aid in order to change the battery. This diverted the others. Potts explained the technology of the device as he stuffed it back in his ear. "Digital, programmed like a computer."

"Does it work?"

"What?"

"Your hearing aid."

"He can't hear you."

Debbie left the paper with them when she rose to go, and Armitage Shanks read the story aloud. Afterward, the question was put as to what would be done to the student Kincade.

"Immediate expulsion," Bingham said with relish.

"He's still here."

"There will have to be a trial." He leaned toward Potts. "A hearing."

Before they left, Debbie returned with the news that the body of a football fan had been discovered in a motel on 31. Death was a touchy topic with the OBs, and they reacted without their customary facetiousness.

"And what was the cause of death?"

"They're calling it a homicide."

"Good heavens."

4 ⟶ SARAH KINCADE WAS BUFFETED BY conflicting emotions. On the one hand, she was proud of the stunt her brothers had engineered and pleased by the reaction of the other women in her dorm. Everyone said that college boys had become too serious, thinking of careers and a remote future before they unpacked as freshmen, moving through the years of study as if they couldn't wait to be out in the real world working their heads off for some silly corporation. What memories could they have of their youth? They hadn't had any. In one fell swoop her brothers had erased that image of the college boy as prematurely serious. In the wee hours, Sarah went with a dozen others from the dorm to survey the scene.

A huge tow truck was parked on the lawn in front of Corby, its wheels having made deep ruts as it was backed toward the building. A chain still dangled from the uplifted derrick in the back of the truck. And there on the ground lay the bronze statue of the Notre Dame priest who had blessed the Union troops at Gettysburg. Her Southern blood thrilled at the justice that had been done.

"What will happen to them?" someone asked, shivering in the early morning air.

"Who did it?"

Sarah held her breath to see if the identification would be made. It was. Her brothers could have had the pick of the excited women ringing their handiwork, but then the two of them had always been shamelessly popular.

"I can never tell them apart," someone said, squeezing her arm.

"Neither can they."

"Can you?"

"Most of the time."

The other girls seemed ready to carry her back to the dorm in triumph.

But another and conflicting emotion returned when she was back in her room. Caleb Lanier. Caleb was everything her brothers were not, serious, an excellent student, searching out professors like his hero Roger Knight as if he feared he wouldn't be worked hard enough by other professors or learn enough from them. And it was his article in the *Irish Rover* that had set her brothers off. If they should actually be expelled because of this, Caleb would somehow be to blame.

It was early in Memphis when she called home to tell her father the news. He was delighted. His sons had succeeded where he had failed.

"Tell me all about it," he urged.

"The boys should do that."

"I tried to reach them last night to get a report on the game. They must have turned off their cell phones."

"Well, they were pretty busy, Dad."

Her father thought it was past time for Notre Dame to set

the record straight on its involvement in the war. He didn't have to specify which war he meant. "The Church is apologizing for everything else. They ought to apologize for this. Imagine, honoring that madman Sherman."

Her mother came on. "Are the boys in trouble?"

"Oh, I hope not."

"Such a strange story in this morning's paper. 'The Writing O'Tooles.'"

"Tools?"

"O'Tooles. A husband and wife, both of whom write. I never heard of either. His book is on Notre Dame. What's odd is that she lives here in Memphis and he writes for a paper in Atlanta."

Why was her mother going on about this?

"Sarah." Her voice had dropped to a whisper. "See if you can get a copy of that book for Daddy. *Irish Icons*. They must have it in the campus bookstore. I'm sure he'd love it."

Sarah promised.

After she had showered, she gathered her golden hair and carefully plaited a single braid. There was a call waiting for her on her phone. It was Caleb.

"Have you been to Mass?"

"No." Another nice thing about Caleb was Sarah's sense that he would keep her on the straight and narrow. "There's a late Mass here tonight. Why don't we have breakfast?"

Everybody seemed to be talking about Father Corby's statue. Not the best topic for them.

"Well, I enjoyed meeting the great Roger Knight," she said.

"Not as much as my uncle Magnus."

"I was never clear who his friend was."

"Oh, they're classmates. I don't think they'd seen one another in years."

"Mother wants me to get a copy of his book for Daddy."

"No kidding."

"Have you read it?"

"Not yet. It's really not much of a book."

"Well, aren't you loyal."

She put a hand on his, and he actually blushed. It was all Sarah could do not to throw her arms around him.

"Want to go see the statue of Father Corby?" he asked.

"When I can sit here sipping coffee with you?"

"I wonder what your brothers thought of my article on Notre Dame and the Civil War."

"What would anyone think?"

"What do you think of it?"

Here was the moment of truth. Loyalty to her brothers, to the South, to the great lost cause, or a little white lie telling Caleb she had loved what he wrote.

"I absolutely loved it."

"You're just saying that."

"Would you like me to sing it?"

"Roger Knight liked it."

Her lower lip puffed out. "What more could you ask?"

5   ON SATURDAY NIGHT LARRY DOUG-
las had to get Crenshaw, the head of
Notre Dame security, to tell Jackson he had to leave his tow
truck right where it was, on the lawn before Corby Hall.

"The hell with that," Jackson said.

Larry had taken the precaution of pocketing the ignition
keys. "Laura will give you a ride," he explained.

"I don't want a ride. I want my truck. I'm in business."

"At this hour of the night?"

"It's Saturday night. This is my big night."

"Jackson, your truck has become evidence."

The uniform was a powerful persuader, usually, but by now
Jackson had to have noticed that Larry's uniform was after all
that of a mere member of campus security. So he had a shield
and handcuffs and a cell phone hanging from his belt; he
didn't have a weapon. Someday he would, of course. Someday,
he hoped, he would be on the South Bend police force, where
he wouldn't have to explain the seriousness of their work to
his colleagues. Crenshaw had been a real cop and taken the
campus job after retiring. He obviously didn't want it interfer-
ing with his retirement.

So it was with some trepidation that he called Crenshaw

and explained the situation. It was a good thing Jackson couldn't hear Crenshaw's side of the conversation. Larry's boss didn't seem to realize that pulling down the statue was an outrage and an investigation would have to be made.

"There should be prints on the steering wheel," Larry explained, speaking so that Jackson could hear him.

"What the hell's the charge?" Crenshaw demanded.

"Stealing a truck, for one thing. Stealing a man's livelihood and then pulling down a statue of one of the great men of Notre Dame."

Jackson seemed placated by this version of events.

"I told him Laura can take him back to his station."

"Why don't you do that?"

Sometimes Larry thought he was the only one in campus security who understood the importance of their function. There was no point in telling Crenshaw that he was in charge of things. Crenshaw would probably insist that he call downtown and turn the whole thing over to the South Bend police. Ten minutes of conversation went by before Larry thought it was safe to let Crenshaw speak to Jackson. Jackson had trouble knowing which end of Larry's new phone to put to his ear, and when he talked into it he practically swallowed it. He had a radio in the truck with which to communicate with the station. Crenshaw, thank God, came through and convinced Jackson his truck would have to stay where it was.

"You own the truck?" Larry asked Jackson.

"If I did, I'd sell the damned thing."

"The university will compensate you for your trouble."

But it was the humiliation of having his truck stolen that sat heavily on Jackson. What ribbing awaited him when he returned without that tow truck?

Larry got on the phone to Laura and told her he had an assignment for her.

"An assignment! I don't work for you."

"Orders from Crenshaw."

"I'm not even on duty, for heaven's sake."

Larry dropped his voice. "As a personal favor? As soon as I clear up matters here, we can get away . . ."

That did it. Get away? When Larry thought of getting away, it was Laura who receded into the distance.

She came, Jackson got into the passenger seat, and Larry thumped the roof over Laura's head. "Don't use the siren."

She did, of course. She was like a kid when it came to sirens. He listened to the plaintive wail fade away down the campus road. Then he turned to the crime scene.

He had already marked it off, with stakes and yellow tape. Little bands of students came to see what had happened, but that yellow border might have been an electric fence. They stayed clear. Larry stepped over it and made a bit of a show of walking around the truck, bending over and checking the tires, and then going to the fallen statue. When he crouched beside it, Father Corby seemed to be aiming that blessing right between Larry's eyes. Larry stood abruptly, reminded of the agony confession had become since he and Laura had gotten back together. She said everything was all right, since they were going to be married and all, but she knew better than that. So did he. But it didn't matter. A woman has an unfair advantage over a man in that department. It didn't help that he felt that Laura was lowering huge coils of rope over his shoulders, pulling it tight, pinning his arms to his sides . . . No, she would want to leave his arms free.

"Hey, you in charge?"

Larry turned to face a tall, bright-eyed boy with a big smile. Red hair appeared when he pushed back his baseball cap.

"You have to keep on the other side of that yellow tape."

"I did it. I want to confess."

"What do you mean?"

"I stole the truck, I pulled down the statue, I'm your man."

With students you had to be careful. Larry didn't want to run the risk of what had happened to Jackson, but the kid seemed serious—a little drunk, maybe, but serious.

"See that squad car on the road? Wait for me there."

That would be the test. But the kid went dutifully to the car and stood there, loudly proclaiming that he had done it all. Larry went to shut him up, put him in the backseat, and drove to the headquarters of campus security. On the way, he called Laura.

"You done yet, honey?"

"I wish I were. Laura, I want you to get back to Corby Hall and make sure people keep away from things until we can make a thorough investigation."

"Larry, I told you before. I'm not on duty."

"Who's honey?" the kid asked from the back.

"Be quiet. You're in trouble."

He called Henry Grabowski and explained the situation to him. Henry seemed delighted by what had been done on campus.

"Look, I need help."

"I'm with Kimberley."

"Bring her along."

"I'll come by the office first."

That done, Larry sat the kid down, pulled out a pad of paper, and said he wanted to hear all about it.

"First. What's your name?"

"Malcolm Kincade."

This was more like it. Larry felt that he was at last putting order into a messy night.

That had been Saturday and early Sunday. Before he got the full statement from Kincade, Henry and Kimberley showed up, and then came Laura, looking daggers at Kimberley. Once, for a brief bright shining moment, Kimberley had gone with Larry, but then Henry had come along and Larry was back with the more ample and amorous Laura. He shagged the three of them off to Corby Hall and completed Kincade's statement.

He turned it in to Iglesias, the guy in charge of discipline, and if he had expected to be congratulated, he would have been disappointed. It was as if he were trying to create trouble for the university rather than control it.

"Good work," Iglesias said, scarcely looking at the report.

"Jackson wants his truck."

Iglesias stared at him. "Is that still on the lawn? Get it out of here."

When Larry called Jackson to say that he was releasing his

truck, his heart wasn't in it. A lot of good an all but sleepless night had done him. Well, at least it had kept Laura at bay.

On Monday, when the body was discovered in the Tranquil Motel out on 31, all the commotion on campus seemed a farce. Larry called Jimmy Stewart, hoping the detective would want to exchange information with a colleague. Geez, he wished he were a real cop.

6 WHEN FATHER CARMODY HEARD
of the body found in the Tranquil Motel
and of possible connections to the university, he asked Philip
Knight to keep an eye on the investigation, on their usual
terms. That was fine with Phil. He and Jimmy Stewart were
old friends. When he got hold of him, Jimmy said he was
heading out to the Tranquil Motel.

"I'll see you there."

"I'll have a rose in my lapel."

There was still talk of Notre Dame going to the Rose Bowl
that year.

Phil got to the motel before Jimmy, but then he was closer;
Jimmy had to come from downtown. He looked into the bar
and got a pretty smile from the woman with PHYLLIS on her
name tag.

"I'm looking for Jimmy Stewart."

"The detective."

"So you know him."

"Are you from Immigration?"

He had her explain that and then wished he hadn't. In the
middle of her rant, she fell silent. Michael Beatty, the man-

ager, entered. He looked at Phil and then the barmaid.

"He's from Immigration," Phyllis said.

Beatty grew alarmed. "What is it? What's wrong?"

Phil took his arm and led him out of the bar. "We think she's a foreign spy."

"Phyllis?"

"If she looked like one, what good would she be?" He punched Beatty's arm. "I'm working with Jimmy Stewart."

"What a terrible thing."

He meant for business, but who could blame him?

Phil saw Jimmy's car pull up out front and went to meet him. "I've been talking to the barmaid. I think she's a wetback."

"It's a wet bar."

They went through the lobby and down a long corridor to 302. There was a plump officer on duty watching the soaps. Jimmy introduced her as Lois Lane, then told her to take a break. From what?

Jimmy shut the door and then showed Phil around the bedroom and the bathroom, bringing him up to speed. When they came back to the sitting room, they sat.

"Okay. She checked in with Mr. Kelly. Only she isn't Mrs. Kelly. Her name is O'Toole, and her husband was in town to sign a book on campus."

"The visitors' book?" Then Phil remembered. "I met him."

"When?"

"Saturday."

"Where?"

"He came by to see Roger."

"He's still here, according to the paper he works for in Atlanta. He stayed in a condo owned by a bunch of newspapers for their reporters to stay in while they're here. You and I are going to give him the bad news."

"Doesn't he know?"

"If he does, I'll want to know how."

"But it's in the morning paper."

"What? That the body of a Mrs. Kelly was found here?"

"Where's Mr. Kelly?"

"Good question. He's a publisher located in Athens, Georgia. His company, that is. He isn't there. He was here for the game Saturday."

There was more. Jimmy had spoken with the guests who had complained about 302. "Some bearded guy spent hours in the bar with the victim. She brought him back here. Kelly doesn't have a beard. At least he didn't have one when he left Athens."

"A busy lady."

"That was the complaint. There's also a student mixed up with it."

"Oh-oh."

"Funny thing. Phyllis in the bar saw the picture of the kid that tipped over the statue on campus and says he's the one."

"Kincade. Maybe I should talk to him."

"We both will. But first O'Toole."

On the way to the condo, Jimmy told him Jankowski's theory of how Madeline O'Toole had died. Smothered. Probably with a pillow. It sounded easy, like drowning, but Phil had never had the experience.

"And you have your choice of interested men."

The condo was east of campus in the town of Mishawaka, a large building whose units were owned or rented by affluent alumni who wanted comfort when they came for Notre Dame games. Some were owned by parents of students, again to make visits more comfortable. Conspicuous consumption.

Jimmy had the manager take them upstairs. His name was Scott Moore, and the request puzzled him.

"No point in causing a fuss."

"What kind of a fuss?"

"We are bearers of bad news."

"You said you were police."

"That's right."

"Is this an arrest?"

"We'll see."

They stood back while Moore knocked on the door. A minute went by. He knocked again. The door opened.

"Someone to see you," Moore said. He looked as if he'd like to hang around.

"I've got to catch a plane," the little man in the doorway said, looking impatiently at Moore and then, beyond him, at Jimmy and Phil.

Jimmy stepped forward. "Are you Magnus O'Toole?"

"Who are you?"

Jimmy showed him his ID. O'Toole backed up as he looked at it, and Jimmy and Phil went in. Phil shut the door, thanking Scott Moore for all his help. Whatever possibility had led Jimmy to think it would be good to have the manager run interference for them had not been realized. Moore made a wet disgusted sound as the door closed on him.

"You're Phil Knight," O'Toole said.

"You better sit down, Mr. O'Toole," Jimmy said.

"I told you, I've got a plane to catch."

"Is your wife named Madeline?"

O'Toole sat down. "I didn't even know she was in town."

"Someone tell you that?"

"Quintin. Quintin Kelly."

"You know him?"

"He's my wife's publisher. She writes novels. Under a pen name."

"I'm afraid something's happened to your wife."

"Happened to her?"

"Her body was found in her motel this morning."

O'Toole rose from his chair like a marionette on strings. His mouth opened. "Quintin," he said.

"Quintin what?"

"I told you. Kelly. They came to South Bend together. He wants to marry her."

"Then he wouldn't want to harm her."

O'Toole began to babble, telling them what a lousy marriage he had, of his wife's stupid novels, of the affair she had apparently been having with Kelly. Kelly had come to tell

114

O'Toole this and get his okay to marry his wife. "He spent Saturday night here."

"I thought he was with your wife."

"He forgot. We were drinking." O'Toole gave his face a dry wash with his hands. "Sunday morning he remembered. He stole my car and went to the Tranquil Motel."

"Where is he now?"

"In the bedroom."

"He came back?"

"They had a fight."

"Let's talk to Quintin Kelly."

When Kelly awoke he looked at O'Toole. "I thought you left."

"These are police."

Kelly looked at Jimmy, then at Phil. " I know you. What's going on?"

"Something's happened to Madeline," O'Toole said.

"She's dead," Jimmy said.

"I told them about your fight with her."

"What fight?"

Jimmy said, "Okay, that's enough. We're all going downtown, and you're both going to tell me what you've been up to these past few days."

"I've got to catch a plane!"

Kelly got his feet onto the floor and rocked himself upright. "What are you suggesting?"

"Downtown."

"Am I under arrest?"

"Let's put it this way: You have no choice."

Obviously Jimmy wanted to talk to the two of them one at a time. He advised them to say nothing until they had a chance to talk to their lawyers.

"I don't believe this," Kelly said.

O'Toole just looked at him and shook his head. "Quintin, Madeline is dead."

7 PROFESSORS WHO PONTIFICATE
in class on the events of the day, cloak-
ing their dubious remarks in the mantle of academic authority, might not be the lowest form of university life, but they
were, in Roger Knight's estimation, certainly near the nadir. It
had become a mark of his own teaching at Notre Dame to
bring to the attention of students relevant items of the institu-
tion's past history of which they might otherwise remain in
ignorance even after four years on campus. Thus he had given
courses on G. K. Chesterton and the great writer's lectures at
Notre Dame on Victorian literature; he had rescued from
undeserved oblivion F. Marion Crawford, also a onetime visitor to the South Bend campus; the nineteenth-century contro-
versialist Orestes Brownson, who was buried in the lower
church in Sacred Heart Basilica, had formed the basis of a
semester's seminar. As for Henry James and William Butler
Yeats, hardly more than allusions to their campus visits were
justified, but in all cases, Roger hoped to instill knowledge of
and reverence for Notre Dame's past. When he embarked on
his current course dealing with Notre Dame's involvement in
the Civil War, he had felt safely lodged in the relevant past.

Now the toppling of the statue of Father Corby after the Georgia Tech game presented Roger with a problem.

The prank, if that was the right word for it, suggested that the bloody and bitter battles of a century and a half ago were no longer sufficiently remote to admit of serene and balanced discussion. The heroic action of Father Corby, at least as enduring as bronze, if not more, had improbably been transformed into an event of current controversy. Chatting with Father Carmody about recent events did little to ease his mind.

"The boy's father tried something similar. Unsuccessfully." The old priest's smile was benevolent.

"Just youthful high spirits?"

"Oh, they're from Memphis, you know. Never forget that."

"The Civil War."

"They would say the second war of independence. When I think of the growth of the government since those days, I sometimes wonder if we won."

Roger's solution was to turn to the priest-poet John Bannister Tabb and make a greater fuss over his verse than it perhaps deserved. After class Caleb Lanier said he wished he'd known what Roger was going to speak of today. "I would have brought Sarah Kincade."

"She likes Tabb's poetry?"

"I think he was some kind of friend of the family."

"Do bring her next time."

He brought her by that afternoon when he noticed Roger's golf cart parked outside his office in Brownson. There were those who wondered how the old building had survived the wrecking mania of recent years. Comparatively new buildings, like the University Club, were scheduled for the wrecking ball, but Brownson was as old as a Notre Dame building could be, and here it was in the third millennium providing office space to those on the lower rungs of the faculty. Roger was housed there because his first-floor office was easily accessible from the parking lot.

He greeted the young couple with delight. "I understand your family knew John Bannister Tabb."

"My mother must have dozens of his poems by heart."

Most of Tabb's poems were short, but even so, this was tribute indeed.

"It's because he was Catholic. A priest. My mother insists that Scarlett O'Hara and her family were Catholic."

"I think she's right."

So they talked of John Bannister Tabb, the scion of a wealthy Virginia family who had been a blockade runner for the South and been taken prisoner.

"He met Sidney Lanier in prison."

But Roger couldn't keep his mind on such lore. Talking with Sarah made it impossible to forget that her brother faced possible expulsion for toppling the statue of Father Corby. Jackson, the man whose truck had been stolen, had identified Malcolm Kincade as the student who had driven off with his vehicle.

"Why did he confess?"

Sarah pursed her lips. "It's a secret."

"Not that he confessed."

"No. Why."

"Oh, come on, Sarah," Caleb said. "You can trust Professor Knight."

"Oh, well, it won't stay a secret."

It all turned on the fact that the Kincade boys were identical twins. Jackson had identified one of them. Soon he would be induced to identify the other as the student who had stolen his truck.

"Only one of them did it, but it will be impossible to say which one," Sarah concluded.

"What an alibi," Caleb said.

8 FEENEY WAS A POLITICAL HOS-
tage in the coroner's office, his accep-
tance of a place on the ballot some years ago the condition of
his father's continuing to be cared for by the local political
machine. This act of piety had blasted his career. After a res-
idency in pathology at the Mayo Clinic, he had been on the
brink of the kind of future he had long dreamt of, a combina-
tion of medicine and research. Instead he had ended in the
coroner's office as assistant to Jankowski, who, like Feeney's
father, was a beneficiary of political largesse. Whenever
Jankowski pretended to the knowledge his position suggested
was his, Feeney faced a problem in diplomacy.

"Smothered?"

This had been Jankowski's explanation of the death of the
woman who had been found in the Tranquil Motel on 31.

"Probably a pillow. There must have been half a dozen pil-
lows on that bed."

Feeney said nothing. Jankowski's theory was a logical possibility, of course, but was hardly compatible with the bruises
on the woman's neck.

Kimberley, Feeney's assistant, was reluctant to assist him
in his professional task, and who could blame her. He

couldn't stand dead bodies himself. So why pathology? The idea had been that he would spend his life examining tissue, doing biopsies, far from the sick, let alone the dead. Besides, Feeney felt guilty for persuading Kimberley to stay on here, rather than continue taking courses at the local campus of Indiana University. Maybe persuasion wasn't the right word.

"I don't want a career," she had said.

How old-fashioned she was. A husband, a home, children, a life as much like her parents' as possible, that was her dream. She was very good with paperwork, what there was of it. Her main function, though, was to provide Feeney with company during the long, boring hours in the morgue. This was selfish. He knew that. At first he had thought that just possibly, despite the seven- or eight-year difference in their ages, romance might bloom in that chilly domain. But Kimberley was deferential and he was shy and nothing happened, and now she had more appropriate admirers: Henry Grabowski and, before him, Larry Douglas.

"What happened to Larry?"

"Nothing happened to him."

"He used to come around."

"That was in the line of duty," she said primly.

As if to give plausibility to her white lie, Larry stopped by to ask what they had learned about the woman who had been found dead in the Tranquil Motel.

"You'll have to ask Dr. Feeney." Kimberley's tone was several degrees below room temperature.

Feeney had followed this exchange from his office.

Kimberley brought Larry in. "You remember Officer Douglas, don't you, Doctor?"

"Sit down, Larry."

"Should I shut the door, Doctor?"

"As you wish."

She shut the door.

"What's wrong with her?" Larry asked.

"Perhaps you've broken her heart."

"Did she say something?"

Good heavens. These were deep waters for Feeney, and he paddled quickly out of danger. "You came to see the corpse?"

"Can I?" How eager he was.

"Of course."

Larry must be on the case. Feeney had learned from Kimberley when she had been interested in Larry that his ambition was to get on the South Bend police. Perhaps Feeney should speak to Casey. The politician owed him a favor for blighting his career.

They had to pass through Kimberley's office on their way to the elevator that would take them down into the morgue. Kimberley affected to be absorbed in her computer.

"We're going downstairs."

"Do you want your calls transferred?"

"Just take messages."

Larry's eagerness seemed to drop with the temperature as they descended, and when Feeney pulled out the drawer and pulled back the cloth that concealed the body, Larry let out a yelp.

"You say she was smothered," he said when he could speak.

"That was Jankowski." The alleged coroner might just as well have said that the woman had died because her breathing had stopped.

"That wasn't it?"

"Look at these bruises."

Larry tried to look from about six feet away.

Feeney told him what those bruises probably meant. "You got the guy who did it yet?"

"Can we go back upstairs?"

Feeney covered the body and slid it away, and they went back to the elevator.

In his office, they settled down, and Larry developed his theory of the case. "The police, the South Bend police, are concentrating on two guys, her husband and her boyfriend. As they should, as they should. I think there may be a campus connection."

"How so?"

Larry had just come from the motel, where he had talked to a woman who tended bar there. "She had been working Saturday night. The woman we just looked at was there. A Southern belle with a tinkling laugh. According to Phyllis, she drew men like flies. One of them was a student. The way it came out was she brought up the incident on campus. Pulling down the statue of Father Corby?"

"I read about that."

"So the kid who admitted doing that was in the motel bar that night. They all scattered after the statue came down, and apparently that's where he went. According to Phyllis, it was like a big reunion between him and Madeline O'Toole. They're both from Memphis."

A complication in the story was that it was some other guy Madeline O'Toole had taken off to her suite. But the kid, Kincade, stayed on in the bar, and then he asked at the desk what her room number was. "Only he asked for Mrs. O'Toole. They said there was no Mrs. O'Toole there. He insisted there was. That's when he asked Phyllis to explain it all to the manager. She told him to talk with the bookkeeper Kitty.

"The bookeeper?"

"Phyllis says she stays late on football weekends."

"Why?"

"To be shocked and scandalized."

"She figured out he meant the woman in 302. And he went down there and began pounding on the door until she came to the door and told him to go away."

There was more. Later still, Kincade and the man who had gone off with Madeline O'Toole to 302 came back to the bar together. "They closed the place."

"So."

Larry pulled on his earlobe. "It's what happened afterward that I'm interested in."

"You figure Kincade went back . . ."

Larry nodded.

"How are you going to prove a theory like that?"

Larry sat back. "That depends on what the lab picked up when they went over the suite."

9   JIMMY STEWART HAD QUINTIN
Kelly put in an interview room and then
sat at his desk looking over the report from the crime scene.
The clothing Madeline O'Toole had hung in the closet suggested that she had come for a week rather than a weekend: a
pantsuit, two dressy dresses, a pair of flats, a pair of heels, and
running shoes to go with the warm-up suit. Had she gone for a
run while registered at the motel? He would check that with
Michael Beatty or, a source with more curiosity, Phyllis. Lin-
gerie, sweaters, two pair of slacks. A purse as well as a kit bag
for cosmetics and the like. Six hundred dollars in the wallet,
along with a deck of credit cards, all of them in the name of
Madeline O'Toole. The list of paraphernalia from the bathroom
and bedroom was lengthy—brush, comb, hair spray, three
hairpins, lipstick, perfume, creams, ointments, on and on. The
glasses and bottle and ashtray had been gathered up as well,
and the bedclothes. Nothing on the list jumped out at him. He
buzzed Officer Hudak and told her to show Mr. Kelly in.

"In your office?"

"That's right." It seemed best to keep the interview on a
less threatening level.

Kelly came in glowering, looked around the office, and

shook his head. "Now what the hell is this all about?"

"Well, whenever we have a dead body we like to seek all the help we can get in finding out what happened."

Kelly sat. "I still can't believe this."

"When did you last see her?"

"When exactly did she die?"

"Mr. Kelly, she was killed."

Again he shook his head.

"Okay. You and Madeline O'Toole checked into the motel on Friday afternoon as Mr. and Mrs. Kelly."

"I suppose they just assumed that."

"You were in the same suite."

Kelly looked away. "Yes."

"None of your things seem to have been in the suite."

"I moved out."

"When was that?"

"Sunday afternoon."

"Why did you do that?"

"That's a private matter."

"Not any longer. You may have been the last one to see her alive. You did see her when you took your things, didn't you?"

He hesitated. "Yes, I saw her."

"To say good-bye."

Kelly sat forward. "Look, I hate to say this about her, but the woman was unstable. Emotionally. She seems to have met every man in the motel."

"There were complaints from other guests."

"I'm not surprised. It could have been any of her new friends, I suppose."

"We like to have a motive. You seem to have a pretty good one. You brought her to South Bend, you were shacked up together—"

"Now wait a minute."

"What would you call it?"

"Oh, call it whatever you want." He looked desolate. "We talked marriage." He might have been describing an abandoned scientific theory.

"I want to be accurate."

"We shared a suite, yes."

"And went to the game together."

"I went to the game. She was living it up in the bar."

"You didn't take her to the game?"

"She wasn't interested in the game."

"So why did she come all the way to South Bend? There must be bars in Memphis."

"I asked her."

"Just to be company."

"Look, I am perfectly willing to be all the help I can."

"Good. I understand you're a publisher."

"Juniper Press."

"In Athens, Georgia."

"Madeline was one of our most successful authors. Her novels weren't literature, but people seem to like that sort of thing."

"What sort of thing?"

"Romance."

"So her death represents a loss to Juniper Press."

"It certainly does." He liked that.

128

"I suppose there was a quarrel when you saw her on Sunday afternoon."

"I wouldn't call it a quarrel."

"What would you call it?"

"I told her what I thought of her."

"How did she react?"

He thought about that. A look of dejection. "As if she expected it."

"Let's go back to Saturday. You went to the game. When did you return to the motel?"

"I didn't."

"You didn't?"

"I ran into O'Toole in the bookstore, where he was signing books. He's a classmate of mine. He's a sportswriter in Atlanta. He invited me to watch the game with him in the press box."

"You just ran into him?"

"Yes."

"Nearly a hundred thousand people, and you just happened to run into Magnus O'Toole."

"I told you, he was signing copies of his book in the bookstore. There were posters."

"Is he one of your authors?"

"Definitely not. His book, if you can call it that, was aimed at Notre Dame fans. I don't publish that sort of thing."

"Just romances?"

"And regional history. Southern history."

"You a Southerner?"

"Macon, Georgia. Originally."

"And now Athens?"

"Yes."

"You say you didn't return to the motel after the game."

"I didn't come back until Sunday, nearly noon."

"Is that when you moved out?"

"Yes."

"Why?"

"I told you."

"You felt she had made a fool of you. What did she think of your not coming back after the game?"

"She had found other things to do."

"Because you had stranded her. Where did you spend Saturday night?"

"At Magnus O'Toole's condo. It's a place where visiting sports people can stay. You've seen it. You found me there."

"You just decided to spend the night with him rather than his wife?"

"We were both pretty drunk."

"Ah."

"And we had things to talk about."

"His wife?"

Kelly puffed up, about to be indignant, then sighed. "Okay. Fine. Here's the story. Madeline and I had fallen in love. We talked of marriage. She and Magnus had drifted apart. Their marriage was beyond repair. She thought he could get an annulment."

"You're all Catholics?"

"Yes."

"So divorce was out?"

"Oh, Madeline would have settled for that."

"Would you?"

"It's a moot point. I must have been blinded. She was a good-looking woman, and lots of fun."

"And a successful author."

"And a successful author. I realize now I really didn't know what she was like. When I found out the way she had carried on Saturday night, I wanted out."

"You went back to O'Toole's condo."

"That's right."

"Did O'Toole know about you and his wife?"

"The point of seeing him was to speak to him about it, about getting an annulment."

"Lucky you just ran into him."

"That's not quite accurate. The point of the trip was to tell Magnus what Madeline and I intended to do."

"You told him?"

"I did."

"How did he react?"

"I told you we had been drinking. It started during the game, and afterward we went to a campus bar, then on to the apartment of Professor Roger Knight."

"Roger Knight."

"Your partner's brother."

Jimmy let it go. "You were drinking together, and you told him you wanted to marry his wife."

Kelly looked as if he would have preferred another description of the confrontation. But he nodded.

"And he had no objections?"

"I wish I could say that I had a clearer memory of that night. Of course he was angry when I told him. I understand that. I was prepared for it. The fact is, he was jealous of his wife's success as a writer. I suppose that's why he wrote *Irish Icons*."

"I would think he'd want to take a swing at you given the circumstances."

"Maybe he did. The thing is, the longer we talked, the easier it got for both of us. Of course, he knew what she was like, and I had yet to find out."

"Which you did when you went back to the motel on Sunday morning."

"More like noon. She was on her way to the noon Mass at Sacred Heart."

"That makes her sound devout."

"A student had come to take her there. He was one of the men she had met in the bar."

"A student?"

"They knew one another from Memphis."

"So you moved out and went back to the condo."

"I had taken O'Toole's rental car. I wanted to get it back to him."

"Was he at the condo when you got there?"

Kelly thought about that. "He showed up after I got there."

"Showed up?"

"He came out of one of the bedrooms, as if he had just woken up."

"You think he was pretending?"

"Right now I don't know what to think. Here was a man who had been told his wife wanted to dump him."

132

"He took that pretty bad?"

"He did."

"Okay, you're back at the condo, moved out of the motel, everything over between you and Madeline. Is that right?"

"It is. I told Magnus what had happened, and we pretty much agreed on the kind of woman his wife was."

"Then what?"

"I sacked out. It had been quite a night, Saturday, and I was feeling pretty low. I slept right on through until Monday."

"So you didn't decide to go back to the motel and murder Madeline."

He leapt to his feet. "What a godawful thing to say."

"Please sit down."

"I'll be damned if I will. I came down here to be whatever help I could. I have done that. I'm leaving."

"I can't let you do that."

"Are you arresting me?"

"You're a material witness to a homicide. From what you've told me, you had a pretty good motive. But forget about that. I'm not going to hold you as a suspect."

"You're damned right you're not."

"I suggested earlier that you might want to talk to a lawyer."

"I don't need a lawyer."

"I hope not."

"Look, I've got a business to run. You can't ask me to just stay around while you carry on your investigation."

"I am asking that. It's not just a suggestion, either."

"This is outrageous."

"Homicide usually is."

"That sounds as if you're accusing me. I've never harmed anyone in my life."

"I wonder if Magnus O'Toole would agree with you."

Quintin Kelly's mouth became a line. He stood and glared at Jimmy. "I am going to talk to a lawyer."

"Good. Where will you be staying?"

"Not at the motel."

"How about the condo?"

"Maybe."

"I have to know."

He said he would be at the condo, if it was all right with Magnus. "I'll ask him."

"You can wait for him here."

10 "YOUR FRIEND'S IN TROUBLE," PHIL
said to Magnus O'Toole.

His mouth formed a little O on his bearded face. "You don't
think that he . . ."

"Don't you?"

"Geez." Magnus raked his beard with his fingers. "I don't
know."

"He's being interrogated now."

"Wow." Magnus's cheeks puffed up, and then he expelled
air. "He was pretty angry with the way she had acted."

"Tell me about it."

Phil had to understand, Magnus said, that he could only
tell him what his old classmate had said when he came back
to the condo on Sunday afternoon. "He said she'd been living
it up at the motel. I can believe it. Sometimes I think she
imagined she was one of the women in her novels." He
stopped. His eyes grew moist. "Whatever went wrong between
us, the woman was my wife."

"She and Kelly checked into the motel together."

"Their plan was to come up here and ask me for a go-
ahead. Can you believe it? What a sonofabitch."

"How long had you been friends?"

"Friends! I hadn't seen him since we were in school together. He was Madeline's publisher. I suppose that's how it started."

"She lived in Memphis?"

"She didn't like Atlanta. She didn't like me, either, not anymore. She said her consciousness had been raised. About gutter high."

"She moved out?"

"Those damned novels brought in tons of money. She was making more than I did. And happy to let me know it."

"That must have been hard to take."

"You married?"

"Not yet."

"What are you, engaged?" He studied Phil as if he were trying to guess his age.

"In my line of work, I run into a lot of arguments against marriage."

"Oh, don't go by mine. There are lots of wonderful marriages."

"But not yours."

"I picked a lemon in the garden of love. That's a song."

"So Quintin Kelly came to you and said, 'I want to steal your wife.' "

Magnus laughed and then seemed to wish he hadn't. "You saw us Saturday night, at your place. By the way, that was a wonderful evening. My nephew had told me what a great professor your brother is. He was right." Magnus paused. "How did you end up on the South Bend police force?"

"I'm a private investigator."

"Come on."

"Scout's honor."

"I'll be darned. So what are you doing down here?"

"I'm on special assignment for Notre Dame."

"Doing what?"

"Making sure that none of what has happened affects the good name of the university."

"That student?"

"What student?"

"Kelly said that a student came to take Madeline to Mass on Sunday, some kid from Memphis whose family she knew."

"Sounds innocent enough."

"With Madeline, you never know."

"She was a practicing Catholic?"

"Let's say she needed practice."

"Did you know she'd be here this weekend?"

"No! I couldn't believe it when Kelly told me the two of them had come up together."

"You had no suspicions?"

"About him? How could I? I didn't know. Not that I was surprised. I mean what surprised me was that the two of them thought I'd give them my blessing. I was supposed to apply for an annulment!"

"You wouldn't do that?"

"If Madeline and I weren't married, no one is. We were married in the Log Chapel, on campus. December 6, 1979." His eyes were moist again.

"A long time ago."

"You can say that again."

"How would you describe his behavior when he returned to your condo?"

"He brought his bags. He'd moved out of the motel. And he told me why."

"Madeline wasn't what he thought she was?"

"I could hardly disagree with his description of her."

"You were both pretty angry with her."

"I'd been angry with her for years."

"But not angry enough to kill her?"

"Are you kidding?"

"You have to understand how this will look to the police. Your wife's playing around with another man, the man comes to you to give you the bad news, your reaction must have been pretty strong."

"How would you feel?"

"I'd probably want to take a poke at him."

"I wish I had."

"But you didn't."

He laughed a bitter laugh. "Suddenly we were in the same boat."

"No hard feelings?"

"I wouldn't go that far."

"So what then?"

"What do you mean?"

"Where are we? Sunday afternoon. How'd you spend the day?"

"I watched a couple of games."

"At the condo?"

"At the condo."

"With Quintin Kelly."

"He flaked out. Went back to bed. I should have done the same. What a night."

"The police are going to think, okay, Kelly's out like a light, you're angry with your wife, maybe you decided to go have it out with her."

"It was too late for that."

"Too late to make up?"

"Much too late."

"It was over."

"Definitely."

"It certainly is."

O'Toole looked at Phil silently. "I fell asleep on the couch, during the Bears game."

"Dozed off?"

"Slept. It was dark when I woke up."

"So you were asleep for hours."

"That's right."

"And you couldn't know if Kelly decided to go back to the motel."

O'Toole looked thoughtful. "I see what you mean."

"But you wouldn't know."

"I'm sure you could find out without my knowing about it."

"Everything will be found out. You can count on it." Not a statement Phil would have wanted to back up. It was far more likely that what had happened to Madeline O'Toole in that motel suite would be added to the long list of unsolved cases police had to live with.

"If he did it, by God he should pay for it."

"It's always hard to imagine that someone would actually kill another person."

"Maybe he didn't mean to."

"Killed her by accident?"

"Did you ever fight with a woman?"

"What's it like?"

"Forget about the marquis of Queensbury. I don't mean you'd hit a woman. Some men do, but I suspect that's rare. No, you spend half your time trying not to hurt her. Meanwhile, she's coming at you with anything she can lay her hands on."

"You're talking about Madeline."

"I'm trying to say that Quintin might have got into a squabble with her and was just trying to defend himself."

"Maybe you should be his lawyer."

"Was Stewart serious when he told Kelly to get a lawyer?"

"I think he meant you both should."

"I don't need a lawyer."

"Don't be so sure. You have to know the police mind."

"I know what I didn't do."

"Who knows what Kelly is telling Jimmy Stewart."

"What do you mean?"

"Well, think of how what you've been telling me would sound coming from someone else."

"The sonofabitch."

"So contact a lawyer."

"Lawyer, hell. I have to get back to Atlanta."

"I think they'll want you to stick around."

"They'd have to arrest me first."

"You can be held as a material witness."

"What do I know that could possibly help?"

"A lot. Stewart is going to have to work out a timeline on the basis of what you two say. There will be a lot of gaps. Falling asleep for hours, that sort of thing. And there should be witnesses at the motel."

"Someone might have seen him there on Sunday night?"

"Or you."

"Hey, come on."

"I'm thinking like a cop."

"Well, then, think of the motel. As you said, the place must be crawling with witnesses."

"With a key, you wouldn't have to go through the lobby."

O'Toole threw up his hands. "Where would I get a key?"

"Kelly?"

"Hey, whose side are you on?"

"The blindfolded lady's."

(11) THE UNIVERSITY ARCHIVES ARE located on the sixth floor of the Hesburgh Library awaiting the day when a building appropriate to the treasures they contain is erected. Meanwhile, it is there that scholars working on some aspect or another of the history of Notre Dame spend happy hours in congenial if crowded surroundings. And it was there that Greg Walsh, assistant archivist, greeted Roger Knight when he had managed to squeeze through the doorway and, once inside, expanded to his usual girth.

"John Bannister Tabb never visited Notre Dame, Roger."

Several scholars turned in surprise to hear the fluency with which Walsh spoke. A debilitating stammer had been the bane of Walsh's existence. He had obtained a doctorate that did not prove to be a ticket to the classroom; at interviews he had been rendered mute. Undaunted, he went on to law school, but once more the stellar grades he had gained in his courses proved to be no entrée to a forensic career. Finally, he had gone into library science and been hired in the archives, where he lived a mute but satisfying existence, arguably more knowledgeable than anyone who came to the archives to do research. Only with Roger Knight did Greg's stammer disappear. It may have been that the enormous weight of the Huneker Professor of Catholic Studies canceled out Greg's impediment. Whatever the reason, Greg spoke with mellifluous ease with Roger.

"I was afraid of that."

"We have a few interesting things, however."

They repaired to Greg's office, where Roger examined the photocopies Greg had prepared for him: some interesting data on the Bull-Pen, at Point Lookout, Maryland, where Tabb had been held prisoner for seven months in 1864–65. It was there that he had met his fellow prisoner Sidney Lanier.

Greg pushed a book toward Roger. "This is Lanier's novel, *Tiger-Lilies*. Do you know it?"

"Not exactly a rousing defense of the Confederacy."

"I wonder if Southerners realize that."

"Oh, I doubt that anyone would have come to the defense of slavery. After the war, I mean."

"Perhaps you're right."

"Did you find anything about the Kincade who attended Notre Dame?"

"There are several in the student body now."

"I mean their father."

"There isn't much."

What there was was a story from the *Scholastic* telling of the cloaking of the statue of Father Corby with a white sheet as a protest against celebrating Notre Dame's connection with the Union cause during the Civil War.

"Did he think Corby was a combatant?" Greg wondered.

"Perhaps he is taking General Polk as the measure." Polk,

an Episcopalian bishop, had been a Confederate general who sometimes conducted services when he wasn't leading troops in battle.

"What will they do to Malcolm Kincade?"

"Father Carmody is intervening on his behalf. As he did his father's. I hope he succeeds in squashing it."

Roger was thinking of Sarah Kincade's confidence as to how her brothers would handle an accusation. Who would be able to say for certain which of the identical twins had been the culprit?

Roger put the photocopies in his shoulder bag, and he and Greg settled into a forty-five-minute conversation. Roger was reluctant to leave, knowing how bracing it was for Greg to be able to speak without a stammer. When he had finally squeezed himself through the entrance, he waited for an elevator. One came, its door slid open, and five occupants looked with dismay at Roger. He waved them on, waiting for an empty car.

Outside, behind the wheel of his golf cart, he set off for Brownson but on the way decided to continue on to Holy Cross House on the other side of the lake to get an update from Father Carmody.

Having seen Roger bumping over the lawn that separated the house from Moreau Seminary, Father Carmody was waiting for him under the portico when he arrived. The old priest got into the passenger seat.

"I assume we're going to take a little spin."

"*Sed tantum dic verbo.*"

Father Carmody pointed westward like a wagonmaster getting under way. No need to say that he wished to visit the community cemetery.

He spent several minutes at the grave of Father Sorin, then paid courtesy visits to other early members of the Congregation. Then he turned and looked to the north over row upon row of identical stone crosses bearing the names and dates of his departed brethren.

"From about the third row after Father Sorin, all the way to the road, are graves of men who died since I joined the Congregation." He glanced at Roger. "I am not suggesting they died *because* I joined. Sometimes I wonder if there will be room here for me when my time comes."

The phrase "the democracy of the dead" came to Roger's mind as he looked over the cemetery and its crosses, all of the same height, no one singled out posthumously as more important than anyone else. The only judgment that counted would be made by one who neither deceives nor can be deceived. The laity are wont to grumble at flaws in the clergy, demanding they meet the higher standard to which they are vowed. But all those rows commemorated the same fidelity to youthful promises, however differently manifested. It was grace and forgiveness, not merit, that this place evoked.

"Young Kincade will get a reprieve," Father Carmody said when they were settled in the cart again. He lit a cigarette and drew on it with relish. "Smoking out here among the trees reminds me of when I was a seminarian." He smiled. "Against the rules, you know. Of course, there was no talk of a smoke-free campus then. Or if there was, it expressed a fear of fire."

Roger directed the cart down the road to the Grotto, where

they said the Angelus, Roger making the responses. Devotion to Mary plays a prominent role in the life of celibates, a fact about which pop psychologists would say many irrelevant things. Roger knew better. Father Carmody was not an unctuous man, nor was he given to pietistic statements, but as they sat there he said, "I love this place."

He meant the Grotto. He meant Notre Dame. He meant the locale of his whole long life.

"What argument did you use?" Roger asked him.

"About the Kincade boy? I said he had a point. I persuaded them there should be a balancing memorial."

"Another statue?"

"John Bannister Tabb. He fought for the Confederacy, you know. He converted later and was ordained. I never liked his poetry."

"Critics have given it very high marks. He loved Edgar Allan Poe."

Father Carmody's news was a relief to Roger. What a farce it would have been if Jackson had been forced to select which of the twins had stolen his truck. It seemed all right to tell Father Carmody of the planned alibi.

The old priest laughed. "I wish now that I had kept out of it."

That night, when Jimmy Stewart came by and he and Phil discussed the investigation into the death of Madeline O'Toole, Roger listened while he looked over the printed list of items taken from the motel suite.

"Hairpins?" he asked.

"They were found on the bed."

The review of what had been learned from questioning Kelly and O'Toole was the focus of the conversation. Working out a timeline of events left gaps.

Saturday. Magnus O'Toole had flown in early that morning, driven to the condo to leave his things there, and then gone on to the bookstore to sign copies of *Irish Icons*.

Quintin Kelly and Madeline had flown in from Atlanta together. In Madeline's purse was her itinerary, indicating she had come from Memphis to Atlanta. Their flight out of Hartsfield had been delayed, so they had not checked into the motel until after noon.

"How did they manage to get reservations on a football weekend?" Roger asked.

The manager had sent Jimmy to the bookkeeper when he asked that question.

"Kitty," Jimmy said. A wry smile. "You should see her, Roger."

"How so?"

The description dwelt on her dated hairdo.

Roger said, "Sounds like Aunt Agatha's, Phil."

Kitty had reluctantly pulled up the records. It seemed the reservation had been made the previous summer.

"So it wasn't a spur-of-the-moment decision?"

Still on Saturday, Quintin Kelly had taken a motel shuttle to the campus, where he found Magnus O'Toole in the bookstore. He bought a copy of *Irish Icons* and arranged to meet O'Toole outside the bookstore when he had finished his signing. They met and went on to the game, watching it from the press box.

"They had a couple drinks during the game," Jimmy added.

After the game, they had gone on to Legends, where they ran into Caleb and Sarah, who had brought them on to the Knights' apartment.

"When did they leave here?" Jimmy asked the brothers.

Neither Roger nor Phil could say. In any case, the two had gone on to the Morris Inn, where Leahy's Bar was still open. More drinks.

"Did they drink while they were here?"

Drinks had been served; presumably the two men had had their share. When they left the Morris Inn, they would have been well on the way to drunkenness. They made it to the condo, where the point of Kelly's looking up O'Toole was further discussed. The two men agreed that O'Toole's first reaction was what one might have expected, but then, eased by alcohol, they achieved a state of camaraderie. O'Toole fell asleep where he sat. Kelly found a bedroom and collapsed.

Meanwhile, back at the Tranquil Motel, Madeline went to the bar-cum-restaurant, where the game was being shown on several screens. There she was joined by a bearded man and later by a student.

"A student?"

"A kid named Kincade. He recognized Madeline because they were both from Memphis," Jimmy said.

"Phyllis saw her leave the bar with the bearded man, apparently to get away from the kid."

"Phyllis?" Roger said.

"A bartender. Phyllis Brickhouse."

"Brickhouse!" Roger cried. "What a remarkable name."

"It's only hers by marriage. She was born Phyllis Llewellyn. I think I'm pronouncing that right."

Later—but how much later?—the student, apparently noticing that he had been deserted, went looking for his older friend from Memphis. He got the number of her suite at the desk and began pounding on her door. It was late enough to anger nearby guests, and calls were made to the desk. The guests, according to Michael Beatty, had described the scenes outside the door of 302 as like something you'd see in a brothel—the fetching lady looking out, a bearded man beside her, a demanding boy in the hallway wanting in.

"I hope you can keep his name out of this," Roger said.

"The bearded man then came out of the suite and led the boy away."

"Does the bearded man have a name?" Roger asked.

"Kelly says he was Rufus James."

"How does he know?"

"That takes us to Sunday."

Sunday. Quintin Kelly awakened from drunken sleep and realized that he had left Madeline alone in their suite all night. He took the keys of O'Toole's rental car and drove to the motel.

"He expected an angry reception. He found Madeline

indifferent to his absence. With evident pleasure, she told him how she had spent her time alone. Not alone. That was when she mentioned Rufus James."

"Rufus James!" Roger cried.

"You know the name?"

"He's a writer with a small but secure reputation. Just one book—" He stopped, sensing that he was stretching the interest of Jimmy and Phil.

"Maybe that's what they had in common."

"I don't understand."

"Madeline is a novelist. A successful novelist. It ruined her marriage, according to Magnus."

This was the first Roger had heard of the literary achievements of Madeline Butler.

"That's her pen name," Jimmy explained.

"I would like to see her novels."

"Are you sure?"

"In the line of duty."

Quintin Kelly had described his reaction to Madeline's account of what she had been up to in his absence as an epiphany. Suddenly he saw her for what she was. It was Madeline's calmness, even contempt, that had proved to be the end of their affair.

"In the midst of the argument, young Kincade showed up to take Madeline to the noon Mass at Sacred Heart. That enables us to place these events."

"Kincade," Roger groaned. "Did he take her to Mass?"

"Yes."

"Her last Mass."

Jimmy and Phil looked at Roger but decided that silence was the best response.

"What then?"

"After they left, Quintin Kelly packed up his things and moved out of the suite."

"Going back to the condo," Phil added. "He wanted to return the rental car."

The two men, rejected husband and disillusioned lover, had discussed Madeline's character at some length, agreeing that she was what she was. That done, Kelly went into one of the bedrooms and went to sleep. Magnus fell asleep watching professional football on television.

"And?"

"This is where things become fuzzy. Both men speak of Sunday as a lost day, devoted to a sleep that lasted until Monday morning."

"Has the time of death been established?" Roger asked.

"Sunday afternoon. Late. The body was not found, as you know, until about noon on Monday. Feeney figured she had been dead maybe eighteen to twenty hours."

That represented the results of questioning Quintin Kelly and Magnus O'Toole.

"What do you think, Roger?"

"It couldn't have been either of them."

Jimmy looked at Phil. They hadn't mentioned that no one at the motel had seen Kelly on Sunday. But Phyllis insisted that she had seen the bearded man around.

"Ah. Rufus James."

"O'Toole has a beard."

"Could O'Toole have slipped away from the condo without Quintin Kelly noticing?"

"Kelly thinks so. He was out like a light and is just guessing, but he's right. It's possible."

"Both men are being held as material witnesses. Kelly has hired Crumley to represent him. O'Toole's newspaper is sending a lawyer from Atlanta."

"So what do you plan to do, Jimmy?"

"Arrest Magnus O'Toole on suspicion of murder."

"Do you think you can get a conviction?"

"I just arrest them, Roger. The prosecutor tries them."

Roger clapped his hands on his knees and looked around brightly. "Who would like popcorn?"

LARRY DOUGLAS COULDN'T BE-
lieve it when Crenshaw, the head of cam-
pus security, told him that the university was dropping all
charges against Malcolm Kincade.

"He stole a truck! He pulled down a statue!"

"He moved a truck from one place on campus to another.
How does that count as theft?"

"You should talk to Jackson."

"The university will compensate him for the inconvenience."

"Is pulling down a statue an inconvenience, too?"

"If the university says it is."

It was typical of Crenshaw that he welcomed the removal of
a problem, by whatever means. He had put in hard years as a
member of the Elkhart police and had taken this job as a
species of retirement. The antics and misdemeanors on campus never rose to the level of the awful things he had once
faced, and he was unlikely to think that parking violations
really mattered. Larry's initial assignment had been to ride a
bicycle around campus wearing a funny helmet, slapping vio-
lation notices under the window wipers of misparked cars. His
zeal had met with reprimands rather than praise.

"Lay off, Douglas. What do you care where people park?"

Laura agreed, suggesting he just enjoy the campus as he wheeled around it.

Finally, he had been transferred to the office and put in charge of maintenance. "The motor pool," Crenshaw had chortled, apparently recalling his days in the army.

The bad part of being in the office was that Laura was there. To call her possessive was like calling a lioness ferocious; she was given to little displays of claiming affection lest anyone not notice the solitaire Larry had reluctantly bought her. This prompted Henry Grabowski to extoll the joys and freedom of the single life. "Don't let her trap you, Larry."

Henry had alienated the affections of Kimberley in the coroner's office after Larry had gotten onto a fast track with her by reciting poetry. It had been his shame, but it became his boast, that he loved poetry rather more than most. He had memorized poems since he was a kid, and held Kimberley enraptured.

All I could see from where I stood
Was three long mountains and a wood.

"What is that from?"

" 'Renasence.' Edna St. Vincent Millay."

"It's beautiful."

"She was just a kid when she wrote it."

Kimberley had asked Larry if he wrote poetry. He put a finger to his lips and closed his eyes. Well, he tried. After Kimberley ditched him for Henry, who had topped him by reciting in French and Italian, Larry labored over some lines.

154

I miss the mirror of your eyes
I long to hear again your sighs

But he couldn't go on. It broke his heart to remind himself of his broken heart. Besides, Laura found the lines and thought they were addressed to her.

"Take her," Henry had said of Kimberley. "She reminds me of a watch my uncle bought in Naples. All face and no works."

He sounded like St. James. Visiting the morgue and seeing Kimberley in the flesh was worse than trying to write poetry. She was as cold as one of the bodies downstairs. His excuse for going there again was to talk to Feeney about the death of Madeline O'Toole.

"You still got the body?"

"They just arraigned O'Toole this morning."

"The husband."

"Yes, and that raises the question of who claims her when the body is released."

"So the husband did it?"

"That's what they say." Feeney's voice was heavy with skepticism. The assistant coroner whiled away the boredom of his days by reading the reports his father had smuggled to him from the detective division.

"You should read poetry," Larry said, raising his voice in the hope that Kimberley in the next office would overhear and remember the days of yore.

"My guess is the student Kincade."

"Why do you say that?"

"He's the last one who saw her alive, for one thing."

Larry sat forward. Kincade. The student who had got off scot-free after stealing a tow truck and toppling the statue of Father Corby, to say nothing of chewing up the lawn in front of Corby Hall when he backed the tow truck across it to the statue.

"What's his motive?"

"The gonads of the young, Larry. I shouldn't have to explain that to you." Feeney's eyes slid toward the outer office, where Kimberley was moving rhythmically about to whatever tune her iPod filled her ears with.

Feeney went on. The boy, still smitten, returns on Sunday morning, to take his lady love to Mass. A perfect ploy. Afterward, they return to the motel suite. They have drinks brought from the bar.

"How do you know that?"

"Phyllis Brickhouse was a classmate of mine at St. Joe's. Her name was Llewellyn then. She brought them drinks. Love and alcohol, Larry. I could tell you stories. Say he misreads her behavior, thinking she shares his passion. He advances, she resists; in a cloud of passion, and angry now, he starts to strangle her, then settles for a pillow, pressing it to that lovely face and snuffing out her life."

"You should write fiction."

"I do the next best thing. What else is an autopsy report but the final chapter of a life?"

Larry's mind was awhirl with thought. A minute later, he rose, said good-bye distractedly, and walked through the outer office without even noticing Kimberley. On the drive to the campus, his thoughts jelled. The police were pursuing an obvious spoor, the aggrieved husband. Larry was not criticizing, you understand; he considered Jimmy Stewart as, if not a friend, a mentor. He dreamt of becoming his colleague. All he needed was some political clout to get onto the force. If he established the validity of Feeney's guess, the assistant coroner could prove to be Larry's way to becoming a real cop. How often had he listened to Feeney's tale of woe, his career as a pathologist broken on the rock of his devotion to his father? His father was the protégé of the notorious Casey, the king of local political patronage. Larry realized that he was humming, and without the aid of an iPod.

At his desk, he got out the campus phone directory and looked up Kincade. There were three Kincades, Sarah, Malcolm, and Eugene. Well, it couldn't be Sarah. The Kincade boys had the same room number in Alumni Hall.

"Where are you going?" Laura asked.

"Out to give a few traffic tickets." He pushed through the door and into the bracing autumn air.

Across the road, Flanner lifted its eleven stories, blotting out a view of the Hesburgh Library. Catty-corner, at the firehouse, they were hosing down a gleaming hook and ladder. Professionals. Larry felt like raising his hand and casting a Corby-like benediction on them. He, too, was a professional. The one serious member of campus security. It was he who had faced the shamefaced indignation of Jackson. What must Jackson think, having the theft of his car regarded as a forgivable prank?

Crossing the campus in the direction of Alumni, trying not to be bumped off the walk by students, he felt his proletarian resentment rise. These kids were on the path to affluence and security, plucked from the masses by the accident of their SAT scores to vegetate here four years before joining the ranks of the elite.

Larry's own SATs had excited Torsion, his advisor at St. Joe's, a few years ago. He urged Larry to pursue his studies after high school. "Apply at Notre Dame."

"I couldn't afford it."

Torsion waved this away as an irrelevancy. "There are scholarships. Anyway, you hedge your bets by applying at IU and Purdue as well."

No one in Larry's family had gone beyond high school; some had not even finished that. His grades and scores were a fluke they did not understand. Take your high school diploma and get a job with a pension as the end of the rainbow, they advised. Larry had applied at Notre Dame—for a job, and had landed in campus security.

When Henry Grabowski came on the job, he had a kindred spirit. Henry was brilliant. Henry had applied to Notre Dame and been turned down. He knew he was smarter than half the student body. He sat in on classes; he read everything; he could recite French and Italian poetry. Larry had made the mistake of introducing him to Kimberley. She had fallen for him like a ripe peach, the sensibilities raised by Larry now addressed by the polylingual Henry. And Larry, like an idiot, had turned to the smothering embrace of Laura for consolation. Like Boethius, he saw it as a death sentence.

As he neared Alumni, he wondered if he should have phoned first. But Laura would have overheard, and he wanted to operate solo. Now it occurred to him that he could knock on the Kincade door and get no answer, this long walk a waste of effort. No. If there was no answer to his knock, he would telephone. If the telephone was not answered, he would make use of the technique Henry had taught him to tap into campus records.

It was the last possibility that he was driven to. He left Alumni and crossed to the law school, sought out a computer cluster, and in a minute had called up the list of the classes Malcolm Kincade was registered for. He checked Eugene Kincade as well and found an identical list of courses. But when he called up one of the courses, he found only one Kincade listed. He pulled up the other courses—with the same result, except that sometimes the Kincade was E. and sometimes M.

"How did you find that out?" Malcolm Kincade asked when Larry finally tracked him down in Legends. The student bar was aroar with noise, television sets adding to the din. The life of the mind.

"It's a matter of record."

"I thought records were private."

"That's why I'm investigating."

"I don't get it."

"We're worried about hackers."

"So you became one." But the kid found it more amusing

than threatening. He explained the way he and his brother registered. "This way only one of us has to go to class. We take turns."

"But then only one of you can get a grade."

Kincade looked at him with a smile. "Maybe we're the hackers you're after. We put both our names down before the final."

They had another beer. Larry liked the kid. At least he treated him as an equal. It was the scratch on Kincade's face that interested Larry. "You realize that you're incriminating yourself, don't you?"

"Not really. Who do you think I am?"

"Malcolm Kincade."

"Not Eugene?"

"Are you Eugene?"

"I'll never tell."

"Where did you get that scratch?"

"From a Georgia Tech cheerleader."

"Not Madeline O'Toole?"

The kid seemed surprised. "Why do you say that?"

"Where did you go after you pulled down Father Corby's statue last Saturday?"

Kincade was no longer amused. Within minutes, he excused himself, leaving half a glass of beer.

Larry finished his, thinking. He was excited. He knew he was on to something. What if he couldn't tell one Kincade from another? That scratch was better than a proper name. He decided that it was time for him to have a talk with Jimmy Stewart, cop to cop. But first he told Henry.

"Cop *ad* cop *loquitur*?"

"I don't know Italian."

Henry's reaction made him hesitate. Maybe he should learn more before he spoke to Stewart. It was then that he had the idea of speaking to Grafton, the reporter.

Phyllis looked at the guy across the bar. He looked like a boy cop. She had talked enough to the police lately. She told him so.

"I understand."

"What do you understand?"

"I was talking to Sean Feeney the other day. Remember him?"

"We were in school together."

"He's now assistant coroner."

"I know. I voted for his opponent." Phyllis looked to left and to right, then leaned across the bar. "The first time I ever voted Republican. I didn't want Sean wasting himself in such a job."

"He's doing it for his father."

"I know that. His father isn't worth it."

"Shame on you."

"Oh, maybe you're right. But he was voted the boy most likely to succeed when we graduated. How could I vote for him as assistant coroner?"

"We're working together on the Madeline O'Toole case."

"I've told you all I know."

"My interest is the student who was here that night. A kid named Kincade."

"What a hunk. If I were a few years younger . . ." Her voice drifted off. She looked speculatively at Larry. "How old are you?"

"In or out of uniform?"

"Don't be nasty. Care for another beer?" The cop was no hunk, but this was a slow night. After all the excitement of police swarming all over the place, the motel seemed suddenly dull. "I'll come around and join you."

"Don't you have to take orders?"

"They can yell if they need me." There were only two or three others in the bar. Phyllis took him to the table that the dead woman had occupied Saturday night. "Of course, she was still alive then." Phyllis sat. He sat. "What's your name, Officer?"

"Larry Douglas."

"You work nights or what?"

"I'm off duty."

"Give me an hour and I will be, too."

Phyllis liked his reaction. She lifted her glass, and he lifted his. They were toasting when Kitty Callendar appeared in the doorway. Her eyes widened when she saw Phyllis drinking with a customer at a table.

"I'll be right back."

"Was it something I said?"

"I just got an order for a manhattan."

Kitty never came all the way into the bar, of course, and she always took her drink back to her office. You knew it was near

163

closing time when Kitty had her farewell manhattan. When Phyllis brought her drink to her, Kitty was fussing with her silly hairdo.

"How do you keep it up there?"

Kitty seemed to be smiling. She had a hairpin between her teeth. She plucked it out and stabbed it into the pile of hair on top of her head.

"Q.E.D., as we used to say in geometry. Where's Green Card?"

"I'll forget you said that."

Sometimes Phyllis thought that Kitty Callendar had a crush on Michael Beatty. It was ridiculous enough to be true.

"Who was that?" Larry Douglas asked when she returned to the table.

"The Wicked Witch of the East. Or is it the West? I forget which witch. She's our bookkeeper."

"So let's go over what happened here Saturday and Sunday."

"What's the point? You got your man, the husband."

"You ever see him around here?"

"I thought it would be the guy she checked in here with."

"Maybe it was."

"So why are you accusing the husband?"

"Maybe it was young Kincade. He was here Saturday night; he came back on Sunday."

"To take Lulu to Mass."

"Lulu?"

"The floozy in 302. Imagine that. After the way she was

carrying on around here, off she goes to Mass like a good girl."

"Some bad girls go to Mass."

"You Catholic?"

"Aren't you?"

"Of course. I went to St. Joe."

"So did I."

Phyllis decided not to ask him when he had graduated. Larry Douglas wasn't a barrel of laughs, but it was a slow night, and who knew, maybe he'd want to take her someplace afterward. Geez. She was getting as bad as Lulu with the big good-looking Notre Dame student.

Larry wanted to know more about what he called the altercation when the Kincade boy had decided to go back and pound on the door of 302.

"He said he wanted to apologize." She laughed.

"For what?"

"You'll have to ask him."

"And there was already a man in the suite with her?"

"They went off from here hours before. He was the man Lulu was drinking with when young Kincade showed up. They had been at it all afternoon. No wonder they wanted to give the kid the slip."

"Is that what they did?"

Phyllis shrugged. "Three's a crowd."

Larry shook his head. "This is some kind of place, isn't it."

"Oh, you know how it is. You meet someone nice, have a few drinks together, one thing leads to another." She moved her glass about on the tabletop, bringing it into contact with his. She lifted her eyes slowly.

"Larry!"

A pudgy lady cop crossed the bar, looking daggers at Phyllis. She came up to the table and put her hand on Larry's shoulder. She might have been making an arrest. There was a diamond on the relevant fat finger.

"What are you doing here?" she asked, but she directed the question at Phyllis.

Phyllis got to her feet and picked up her drink. Was this how Lulu had felt when young Kincade came pounding on her door?

"Well, Officer, I've told you all I know."

"This is Laura."

Phyllis just nodded and drifted off behind the bar, feeling more foolish than she had in years. It didn't make a lot of sense, but she blamed Sean Feeney for her embarrassment. She had half a mind to give him a call. Maybe he thought Brickhouse was her married name. But it was her mother who had married again and had insisted that Phyllis adopt her new name.

"No one can spell Llewellyn."

14   ARTHUR BENESTAD CRUMLEY SAT in on the arraignment of Magnus O'Toole before meeting with his client, Quintin Kelly.

"Who recommended me?"

"I just picked your name from the yellow pages."

Crumley sat hunched over the table, his head seeming to be just emerging turtle-like from his torso. He wore his glasses on the tip of his nose, the better to peer over them. Practicing before a mirror, he had decided that this over-the-glasses look conferred a kind of shrewdness, even wisdom, on him. It made him look like that idiot senator from Michigan. He said nothing for a moment. Pauses, stretches of silence, were part of his forensic manner.

"I'm surprised they didn't arraign you."

"That's ridiculous."

"It's a better case than they can make against O'Toole."

"I thought you were my lawyer."

"This is just a preliminary conversation." He was going to make this guy squirm for making that crack about the yellow pages. Crumley knew for a fact—well, an alleged fact—that Jimmy Stewart had recommended him.

"Maybe I should get someone else, if this is your attitude."

Pause. Crumley realized that he didn't like Kelly. Nothing special about that, of course, He didn't like many people. "The best defense is to know the offense."

"What I would like you to do is to make them let me leave town. I have a business to run."

"So do the police. So does the prosecutor. You're a material witness."

"I've told them all I know."

"There are gaps."

It all came down to which of the two, Kelly or O'Toole, had slipped away from the condo on Sunday afternoon while the other was sleeping. As far as Crumley was concerned, Kelly had a stronger motive for sending that high-flying lady on her way to the next world. He had said as much to Fauxhall, the deputy prosecutor.

"What evidence do you have that O'Toole was even in that motel suite?"

"A bearded man was seen around there Sunday afternoon."

"You and I could grow a beard."

"O'Toole already had."

"Have you located Rufus James?"

"Are you representing O'Toole?"

"I wish I was." Were? Whatever. But he was stuck with Kelly, who had checked into the motel with the departed lady, whose prints were all over the suite, who had managed to slip away Sunday morning in O'Toole's rental car and go to the motel to have a fight with his beloved.

Now he asked Quintin Kelly what he knew of Rufus James.

"He's a writer."

"And you're a publisher."

"Not his."

"But you published Madeline O'Toole."

"She wrote as Madeline Butler."

"She and James seem to have hit it off in the motel bar."

"And in the suite. She took him back there. I can't imagine what they had in common."

Crumley pushed his glasses to the bridge of his nose and then let them slide down again. If Benjamin Evans, the lawyer from Atlanta, knew his trade, he would hire someone to find Rufus James pronto. Get him anywhere near the Tranquil Motel on Sunday, and the case against O'Toole would evaporate. The jury would have their choice of bearded men, and James, unlike O'Toole, could be placed in the motel, and in suite 302, on Saturday night.

"I will insist to the prosecutor that you have to get back to Athens."

"Good."

"It won't be easy."

Actually, Crumley had already won that argument with Fauxhall. Now he wished he had lost.

"Where are you staying?"

"In the condo."

"As O'Toole's guest?"

"He doesn't own the place, you know."

15 GRAFTON PULLED THE BELT OF his Burberry topcoat tighter when he got out of his car in the parking lot of the Morris Inn. Malcolm Kincade had agreed to meet with him when Grafton said he wanted to do a piece on the motive behind pulling down the statue of Father Corby last Saturday.

The young man was waiting for him in the lobby. Grafton recognized him from his picture in the *Observer* Larry Douglas had given him; he had also pulled up his Web page on the Notre Dame site. It featured a fluttering Confederate flag and a picture of Lee in profile, looking like the man on a cigar box.

"You the reporter?"

"Malcolm Kincade?"

"Eugene."

"I thought your name was Malcolm."

"That's my brother. He's in class."

"Can you tell me about pulling down the statue?"

He clapped Grafton on the shoulder. "I was there. It was a family project. Let's go outside."

Outside, there were tables, an expanse of lawn, and a large white tent at the end of the canopied walkway that started just beyond the table where they sat. Grafton got things going by mentioning that he was a bit of a Civil War buff himself.

"North or South?"

"Both."

"Well, that's better than siding with the Union. That's what Notre Dame did. When my daddy was a student here and found that out, he nearly went on back to Memphis."

"Your father was a student here?"

Kincade pulled a folded piece of paper from his pocket, unfolded it, and laid it on the table. It was a photocopy of an old photograph showing the statue of Father Corby draped in a white sheet. The boy grinned expectantly when Grafton looked up from the photograph. "My daddy."

"So it's a family tradition."

"It is!"

"What are they going to do to you? And your brother?"

"Nothing." He looked disappointed.

"I understand there are plans to put up a statue of John Bannister Tabb."

"That's a start. Most everybody around here thinks the war was about slavery." He shook his head. "That was only an excuse, and it wasn't made until the war was a year and more old. The South was fighting for the Constitution."

"Which one?"

"The original. The one written largely by Southerners."

Grafton made notes, wondering what kind of a story he could make of this. An essay on the War Between the States would get hoots of laughter at the *Tribune*, and Grafton had

had too much trouble becoming a regular reporter to want to run that risk. He decided that any story here lay in young Kincade and his twin brother.

Kincade had pulled out a copy of the *Irish Rover*, an alternative student paper. This was a story about Notre Dame during the Civil War.

"Who is Caleb Lanier?"

"A good man. Just misinformed."

Kincade seemed to think that Father Corby should have crossed the lines and blessed the Southern boys, too, before the Battle of Gettysburg was fought.

Grafton listened and went on writing. After a while he got out his camera and took some shots of Kincade. He thought of taking Kincade over to where the statue of Father Corby had been replaced on its base, but he had pretty much lost confidence that he was onto something newsworthy.

"Was it you or your brother who was out at that motel Saturday night?"

"Why do you ask that?"

No point in telling the young man the story he had heard from Larry Douglas, one he had concocted with Sean Feeney, the assistant coroner. Magnus O'Toole had been arraigned for the murder of his wife, so the idea that the Kincade boy would be accused of anything seemed fanciful.

"Just asking."

"No, tell me."

So Grafton told him. The young crusader's ardor was dampened by the thought that someone might actually think that he, or his brother, had killed a woman, a Southern woman, a woman from Memphis, and Grafton realized that he himself was taking pleasure in seeing the worried look on the young man's face.

"They already arrested the man who did it."

"O'Toole has been arraigned, yes. It's a ploy that's often used."

"How do you mean?"

"Pretend that the investigation is over, lull the other suspects into carelessness."

Kincade frowned.

16 ➤ "I'M NOT A MURDERER," MAGNUS O'Toole had begun when he was led in to meet Benjamin Evans, the lawyer the paper had sent up from Atlanta.

Evans looked like a choirboy and dressed to look older than he was. Magnus was not cheered by the thought that his fate was in this lawyer's hands. Evans took off his topcoat, hung it up carefully, then unbuttoned and rebuttoned his double-breasted suit jacket. "The charge is homicide."

"What's the difference?"

"Years and years." Evans sat down and drew a long yellow legal pad from his briefcase and placed it on the table. He shifted it around a bit to get it right. "So let's begin."

"I didn't do it."

"That's axiomatic. I want you to give me as complete an account of the relevant days as you can."

Magnus felt his heart sink. It was difficult to forget the nice conversation he had had with Philip Knight when he thought they were looking for ways to pin Madeline's death on Quintin Kelly. He felt that he had been tricked into saying things that could later be twisted to mean what he hadn't intended. He said as much to Evans.

"Who is Philip Knight?"

"A detective."

Evans ran his hand carefully over a head of hair that looked as if it had never been mussed. "A detective on the South Bend police?"

"No."

"Excuse me a moment."

Evans stood and left the room, leaving Magnus to feel miserable. There was a Bible in the holding cell, and he had begun reading the Book of Job. He stopped when it seemed to be about himself.

Evans came back. "There is no South Bend detective named Philip Knight."

"He's a private detective. His brother teaches at Notre Dame."

Evans regarded this as irrelevant, so Magnus told him of how he and Kelly had gone to the Knights' apartment after the game last Saturday.

"A social evening?"

"Yes."

"And subsequently Philip Knight interrogated you?"

"I thought we were just talking. They acted as if Kelly was the one they were after."

"They?"

"Knight and Jimmy Stewart."

"Very irregular." Evans spoke with some satisfaction. "And did Jimmy Stewart interrogate you as well?"

"He said he would wait until you got here."

Evans nodded. "Let's regard this as a rehearsal for that

interrogation. I shall want to have this over and done with as soon as possible."

"Good."

But if his hopes had risen, they sank again when Evans sat in while Jimmy Stewart went over the events of last Saturday and Sunday.

"Who is Philip Knight?" Evans said to the detective.

"Why do you ask?"

"My client tells me that someone called Philip Knight, representing himself to be a detectve, interrogated him about these events."

"Interrogated him? When was that?"

"When you were talking with Quintin Kelly," Magnus broke in. "Philip Knight and I came into a room like this—"

"And talked."

"He asked me questions."

"Talking often involves questions. What exactly is the point of bringing this up?"

"I want to establish that my client was misled into thinking that he was talking with a member of your police force. I want to establish that nothing he may have said to this Philip Knight can be regarded as having been said."

"I can certainly agree to that."

Evans sat back in surprise. "But you acknowledge that Philip Knight quizzed my client?"

"I wasn't privy to their conversation." Stewart turned to Magnus. "You were good enough to come down here when I brought in Quintin Kelly for questioning. While I questioned him, you and Knight kept out of the way. You say you had a conversation?"

It dawned on Magnus that Evans was after a technicality, but what would it gain him if he found it? Here the three of them sat in order that Jimmy Stewart might conduct an interview with him, his lawyer being present. Any conversation he might have had with Philip Knight was neither here nor there. Stewart couldn't agree more. So Evans had won an uncontested point.

Evans did better when he interrupted Jimmy Stewart to ask if there was any physical evidence suggesting that his client had been anywhere near the scene of the crime.

"You will be in possession of everything we've found if this goes to trial."

"Is that a yes or a no?"

"Neither."

Evans began a disquisition on the principle of contradiction but stopped himself. "What I presume interests you in my client is that he has been involved in an unhappy marriage. His wife has set up residence in another city; she apparently had been conducting herself in a way that events of the past weekend have made clear. Stewart, you could learn that my client has expressed outrage at what his wife has done, that he is understandably angry with her. He might even have said he'd like to wring her neck."

"I never said such a thing."

Evans displayed a palm. "All that and more you might have learned. I am painting as dark a picture as I can. But you are investigating a murder in a motel where my client has never been."

"Is that so?" Stewart asked Magnus. Evans sat forward.

Magnus looked at both men. "Only once."

Evans jumped to his feet and looked sternly at Jimmy Stewart. "I gather from your reaction that what Mr. O'Toole has just said comes as news to you."

"Not really."

It went on like that. When at last Stewart left and Magnus was alone with Evans, the lawyer looked at him reproachfully. "You should not have told him that you went to that motel on Sunday. Not that it matters. He would have to establish it on some basis other than your unguarded remark."

Alas, that is what happened. Phyllis Brickhouse had seen a bearded man go from a car in the parking lot to a secondary entrance of the Tranquil Motel on Sunday afternoon, perhaps at three or four o'clock. On the basis of that, Magnus O'Toole was arraigned, accused of bringing about the wrongful death of his wife, Madeline.

"Wrongful?"

"At least it isn't an accusation of murder."

"That wasn't me she saw."

"Why do you say that?"

"I was there at maybe one thirty, and I didn't park in the lot."

"We may have to prove that."

Magnus wanted to tell Evans all about his visit to Madeline Sunday afternoon, but the lawyer put him off.

"I will make very short work of his witness."

Magnus was taken away, and in his cell went back to the Book of Job. He was glad that he had mentioned going to the motel to confront Madeline with what Quintin Kelly had told him. He had expected an angry confrontation, but all she wanted to talk about was Rufus James.

"He told me he can get me a better publisher, a New York publisher."

"For your stuff?"

"Magnus, he told me a secret. He writes thrillers under a pen name." She whispered this. "Now don't tell a soul. I think he was sorry he told me."

And so he had driven back to the condo, where he found Quintin still asleep in a bedroom. Magnus had left the television on when he left, muted, and for a moment he stood looking at the screen. He sat on the couch. The game would be a soporific. And it was. In minutes he was sound asleep.

17 ROGER WAS READING *DIXIE COUP* by Rufus James with a fascination verging on disbelief. The attempt to tell of the disintegration of a Southern family in the wake of Appomattox while keeping the story locked in the mind of a retarded eleven-year-old girl who was also mute would have challenged Faulkner himself. The language of the book was apparently a mode of communication one could imagine being invented by someone who had never heard the sound of another human voice. Or perhaps one couldn't imagine that. It was difficult to keep disbelief suspended, and the author seemed to challenge the reader more and more as the novel progressed—if progress be defined by the sequence of natural numbers to be found at the bottom of its pages. Not to finish the book would have seemed a moral fault to Roger, as if he had abandoned a Lenten penance. The obligatory sexual scenes ranged from self-abuse through rape to bestiality, and it was these that critics had praised to the skies, a judgment Roger neither shared nor wished to contest since that would have required dwelling on them.

It was of course absurd to hope to catch the flesh-and-blood author of a novel peeking through his prose. The most imaginary character in any novel is the one that is not in it but writing it. Nonetheless, Roger found himself wondering what sort of fellow Rufus James was. As an author, he made few concessions to the ordinary expectations of a reader. Indeed, the novel might have been written in order to show that a novel that violated all the canons of fiction could be written if not enjoyed.

From time to time, Roger had to come up for air, and he would lay aside the book and think of the odd events at the Tranquil Motel in which Rufus James had been involved. Phil and Jimmy Stewart seemed content to let the outcome rest in the hands of Fauxhall. Granted that Madeline had given Magnus motive enough to do her in, his link to the scene of the crime consisted in the fact that a bearded man had been seen in the vicinity of suite 302 more or less at the time of Madeline's death.

"Surely his lawyer will point out that Rufus James has a beard." As it happened, the photograph of James on the dust jacket of his novel showed a clean-shaven face, but then the novel was nearly a decade old.

"O'Toole admits he was there Sunday afternoon, Roger."

"He does?"

"When Jimmy was questioning him, he said he was there."

"In the presence of his lawyer?"

"Not that it matters." The statement could hardly be used in the trial, but there was an eyewitness.

"Phyllis Brickhouse? She said she saw a bearded man."

Phil was engaged in peeling an orange in such a way that the skin came off in one piece. That was on a par with Roger's doing the *Times* crossword with a ballpoint pen. What other eccentricities awaited them?

"Would they let me talk with Magnus O'Toole?"

"As long as you don't represent yourself as a South Bend detective."

Phil tried to make a joke of it, but he had not liked the suggestion made by Benjamin Evans that there was something underhanded about the conversation he had had at headquarters with Magnus O'Toole. After all, O'Toole knew who and what he was. Not that they were just passing the time while Jimmy questioned Quintin Kelly.

Phil drove Roger downtown and took him to Jimmy's office to arrange for a visit with the accused Magnus O'Toole.

"I'll stay here with Jimmy," Phil said, perhaps mindful of Evans's interpretation of his own talk with O'Toole.

Roger was led away by an officer. As they approached the visiting room, the door opened, and a dapper little man emerged. He stopped and stared at Roger.

"It's all me," Roger said with a smile. "Roger Knight." He put out a hand, which Evans examined as if for fingerprints before taking it.

"Benjamin Evans. I understand you want to talk to my client."

"I'd like to talk with you as well."

Evans looked at his watch like the rabbit in Alice.

"About Rufus James. If I were you, I would make every effort to get in touch with that man," Roger advised.

"I shall be talking to him within the hour."

"Good. Good. Is he still in town?"

"He is holed up in a motel near Niles."

"Holed up?"

"He's a writer."

"I know." The thought that another novel like *Dixie Coup* was in the works was not cheering. "He could very well be your client's alibi."

Evans gave him a prim little smile, nodded, and went off down the hallway. Obviously, it was that possibility that explained the lawyer's locating James.

Magnus O'Toole seemed delighted to see Roger when he came into the room and found the massive Notre Dame professor seated precariously on a chair of inadequate size.

The conversation understandably began with the topic of Rufus James. O'Toole had been informed by Evans that he had located the author and was certain that producing him at the trial would counter any effect the testimony of Phyllis Brickhouse might have on the jury. Indeed, Evans was hopeful that the second bearded man would dismantle the case against O'Toole.

"But you yourself went to the motel on Sunday afternoon?" Roger asked O'Toole.

"I didn't kill her."

"I'm sure you didn't."

O'Toole looked as if he might weep. "I can't tell you how good it is to hear someone say that. Evans acts as if he were engaged in getting a murderer off on a technicality."

"He told me James is up in Michigan writing."

"Have you read any of his novels?"

"I am reading one now. I believe it is his only one."

"Apparently not. That seems to be why he and poor Madeline hit it off."

"I don't understand."

So Roger heard of Rufus James's bibulous confession to Madeline that he, too, wrote trash. Under a pen name, of course.

"He even offered to interest his publisher in taking on Madeline. With the prospect of more money. That's what we talked about. Think of it, our last conversation, and all we talked about was her damned career."

Again O'Toole looked as if he might weep. Who knew what had led him to seek out his wife last Sunday afternoon? A reconciliation? Roger did not dare to ask. Marriage was more of a mystery to him than it is for those involved in one.

He left O'Toole with the confidence that the man would soon be free. When the Knights arrived home, the phone was ringing as if it had been doing so since they left. It was Father Carmody with the news that Malcolm Kincade had confided to Grafton that he had murdered Madeline O'Toole. The young man and the reporter must have arrived at headquarters while the Knight brothers were there.

PART FOUR

1 PHIL WENT TO HOLY CROSS HOUSE to fetch Father Carmody, and the three of them discussed this strange turn of events over dishes of Roger's lasagna.

Roger thought he understood what had happened. "It's a ruse, Father. Obviously, Grafton had convinced young Kincade that his brother was now the prime suspect in the murder of Madeline O'Toole."

"A Notre Dame student confessing to murder!" The reputation of the university was dearer to Father Carmody than his own, and he felt anguished by the prospect of the local, and doubtless national, media bringing the story to the four corners of the country. "One should never underestimate the animus against Notre Dame. Think of the Heisman Trophy." Father Carmody was certain that Brady Quinn had failed to win this award because of anti–Notre Dame prejudice among the voters.

"What do you mean, ruse?" Phil asked.

"I told Father Carmody how the twins were going to handle it if any real trouble developed over pulling down the statue of Father Corby. You can bet that the other Kincade will shortly confess to the same crime. No witness will be able to tell them apart."

"That's crazy!"

Father Carmody apparently didn't think so. A little smile formed on his lips. Did he imagine that such a ruse would put the intelligence of Notre Dame students on display?

Phil, too, began to see it as a joke rather than a problem. "Which twin has the Toni?"

Father Carmody looked blankly at Phil. Of course he wouldn't remember that advertising slogan of years before. Who would?

"Toni?"

"It was a home permanent," Phil told the priest. The explanation didn't help, so he dropped it. "One identical twin as alibi for the other."

The amusement value of the Kincade confession was considerably diminished when Fauxhall, deprived of Magnus O'Toole as his suspect—Evans had rousted out the judge who had arraigned O'Toole and won a quick dismissal—started leaning on Jimmy Stewart to make the case against Malcolm Kincade.

Jimmy had not found the prospect of the second twin coming forward amusing when Phil warned him of what might be in prospect. "I'll charge them both."

"Not with the same murder."

Phil returned to police headquarters with Father Carmody with the intention of speaking to young Kincade. The assignment the old priest had given him when the toppled statue of Father Corby had been the center of events had been reactivated now that Kincade had confessed to the murder of Madeline O'Toole.

"What possible motive could he have had, Jimmy?"

"Ask him."

Some ten minutes later, Phil and Father Carmody were in a visiting room with an insouciant Malcolm Kincade. The young man did not have the look of someone who had confessed to murder. There was a twinkle in his eye, and he had a way of mussing up his red hair as they talked.

"Did you know my father?" he asked Father Carmody.

"Of course. I haven't seen him for some time."

"He's flying up."

"Son, you didn't kill that woman, did you?"

"Why would I confess if I didn't?"

"How do we know you're Malcolm and not Euguene?"

Kincade got out his wallet to show Phil his Notre Dame ID card. Malcolm Kincade.

"How do I know this is your card and not your brother's?"

"Why would I have his card?"

"Malcolm, I know what you and your brother intended to do if things got sticky because of what you did Saturday night."

"Tell me."

Phil told him. "Look, this isn't just a campus stunt. A woman has been killed. I wouldn't be surprised if they hauled your brother in and charged him as well as you."

Kincade grinned. "There are lots of people who were with Malcolm when all this happened."

"Malcolm?"

"Eugene."

So the trickery had already started. Phil would have been angrier if he could believe this young man had actually killed Madeline. He asked him how he had done it.

"It's all in the paper."

"Son," Father Carmody said, "why do you think your brother is in trouble?"

"My brother?"

"That's why you're doing this, isn't it? Who convinced you that your brother was a prime suspect and needed rescuing?"

Later, when they were leaving, they had the unnerving experience of seeing the clone of the lad they had just been talking to brought in, under arrest. Jimmy Stewart was mad. Father Carmody went up to the boy as he was being booked.

"Malcolm?"

"Eugene."

"Where did you get that scratch?"

2 THE SCRATCH ON YOUNG KIN-
cade's face was featured in the exclu-
sive story Grafton had written informing his readers that
relentless and intrepid investigative journalism had enabled
him to solve a case that had been causing consternation
among local law officials for many days. He described the
thinking that had led him to young Kincade. Of course, it
was common knowledge that Kincade had been in the bar of
the Tranquil Motel on Saturday and that he had returned on
Sunday to take Madeline O'Toole to the noon Mass at Sacred
Heart Basilica. No need to mention the role that Larry Douglas and, indirectly, the assistant coroner Sean Feeney had
played in his thinking. Much of the story was cast in dia-
logue form, with your reporter putting a series of questions
to young Kincade that had finally persuaded the young man
that he was the prime suspect in the murder under investigation.

This called for a digression in which Grafton mused on the
morality of stating the matter as he had. There were doubtless
readers who would question the way he had purported to be
conveying to Kincade the current state of the police investiga-

tion and the at-the-time fanciful suggestion that young Kincade was now the target of the investigation. To allay such misgivings, Grafton reviewed the steps in his thinking that had led him to the conviction that young Kincade was indeed the culprit.

First, there was the madcap incident on campus, pulling down the statue of Father Corby with the aid of a stolen tow truck. Such antics had suggested to him not the playful misbehavior of the young but a deep character flaw that could manifest itself in even more serious ways.

Second, there was the fact that the young man had fled to the Tranquil Motel, where in the bar he had met a woman he knew from Memphis, Madeline O'Toole. How much had the young man had to drink before going to the motel? Jackson, the aggrieved owner of the purloined truck, had described the young fellow who had wheedled him out of the cab and then hopped in and driven off in the truck as having "a snootful." Many readers would perhaps recognize the term. It was certain that he had added many drinks to the sum he had consumed last Saturday during the convivial reunion with Madeline in the bar.

Third, there were the complaints of other residents in the motel, roused at an ungodly hour by Kincade's pounding on the door of the woman who had captivated his inebriated heart. An exchange Grafton characterized as warm, promising, and whispered had gone on before she persuaded the boy to go.

Fourth, he was back the following day with the preposterous suggestion that he take her to Mass on campus. Doubtless the police would determine where in fact the infatuated lad had taken the older woman after picking her up on Sunday just before noon. Not even the resilience of youth would have overcome so soon the effects of all his drinking the night before into the wee hours. It was a smitten, headstrong youth who would not be denied that Grafton put before his readers.

Confronted with these facts, as well as others that would be developed in subsequent articles, young Kincade had broken down and confessed to your reporter. Fortunately, he was persuaded that the only honorable thing to do was to turn himself in. Grafton had accompanied him to police headquarters.

The pride of authorship rivals that which caused the fall of the angels. Before his article appeared in print, Grafton had read it over again and again on his computer screen. Once it was in print he could read it through the eyes of subscribers and feel the power of what he had laid before his readers. How could he not dream of what might now come his way as a journalist? For years, he had scrounged around the paper, doing odds and ends, largely obituaries, in the pressroom but not of it. Persistence had paid off at last. And now, with this story, any hesitation that there had been in hiring him would be definitively swept away.

Larry Douglas, of course, was sarcastic in his praise. "Thanks for mentioning where you got the idea."

"I wasn't sure you wanted your role revealed."

"You could have asked."

"I will feature your part in the follow-up piece that will appear tomorrow."

Larry Douglas lit up."You mean it?"

"If a source permits it, of course I will name him. How about Sean Feeney?"

"I can't speak for him."

"Of course not."

"I liked the way you handled the scratch."

Grafton could have hugged him. The suggestion that the overpowered and frantic Madeline had raked Kincade's face with her nails in an effort to defend her honor had been unmistakable in his account and yet oblique. The mark of Cain was on the boy. The scarlet letter.

"Should I mention your fiancée as well?"

"No, don't do that." He looked away. "Laura is shy."

With a gesture, Grafton conveyed to Larry that his fiancée's reticence would be fully respected by him.

"It's just a trial engagement anyway."

"I understand."

"I wish Laura did."

Grafton loitered at headquarters; at the paper he walked among his colleagues as if lost in thought. From time to time, he would take out his cell phone and carry on imaginary whispered conversations with his far-flung sources. South Bend seemed too small a stage for one of his talents. Before leaving, he talked to the girl who edited the paper's Web page, to make certain his story was displayed prominently there. Who might not read it in its now global availability? The thought was dizzying. At the round earth's imagined corners his story would be read on monitors—in England, France, Germany, Italy. Upward-bound lads in Third World countries would gaze at their monitors. Who knew what ambitions would be awakened?

3   ➤   TALK AT THE OLD BASTARDS' TABLE
in the University Club dining room cen-
tered on what Armitage Shanks sardonically called the Romu-
lus and Remus caper. The Kincade twins had been the toast of
the campus after the toppling of the statue of Father Corby. It
was not that rebel sentiment in the historical sense ran high
among the student body, but a brash and daring deed, and one
that ran the risk of expulsion, commanded fairly universal
respect. But now both twins apparently were in deeper trouble, and the mood was more ambiguous. Ambiguity was of
course a constant at the OB table.

"How can one murder have two murderers?" asked Potts.
"It violates the principle of causality."

"Have you ever heard of several people pushing a car?"

"Has the tow truck been returned?"

Grafton's story had been subjected to close and critical
reading by the occupants of the table.

"Baroque," grumbled Plaisance. "The man could write for
the *Jupiter*."

Clarification was demanded.

"Don't you know Trollope?"

A reminiscent expression came over the face of Armitage Shanks. "'Marriage has many pains, but celibacy has no pleasures.' Johnson."

Bingham was reminded of Chink Johnson, who had played hockey in Minneapolis before the war.

"The Civil War?"

"That is a contradiction in terms."

It was the contrast between the apparent Southern romanticism behind the grounding of Father Corby and an admission by one of the twins that he had killed a Southern belle from Memphis that did not sit well with the table. The death, even of a stranger, brought on a lugubrious mood.

Debbie, the hostess, pulled up a chair and joined them. She explained the current theory about the twins. After one of them confessed, the other would come forward to say that he had done it. The result would be a legal impasse. Bingham, late of the law school, waxed indignant at this assault on the sanctity of the law.

"Tell it to O. J.," Debbie advised.

"I'm drinking gin and tonic."

Debbie flagged down their waitress, and another round was ordered.

"Prosecute them both."

"One has an alibi."

"Which one?"

"That is the problem."

"The husband has been released," Potts observed.

"What was the charge?"

"He had written a book."

"They should arrest this Grafton." Shanks fluttered the pages of the local paper.

The father of the twins had arrived in South Bend from Memphis and had objected to Grafton's tendentious account. He was threatening to sue.

"Nonsense."

"The license of the press."

"It all turns on the scratch on the boy's face."

"His brother also has a scratch."

"Hang them both," Bingham said.

"Better well hung than ill wed," Shanks mused.

"Johnson?"

"Shakespeare. A translation from the German translation."

"You're making that up."

Bingham sat forward and began to tell of a precedent in the law, but only Potts paid attention, and he couldn't hear.

"Someone murdered that woman," Debbie said sternly. "They've turned it into a joke."

4 FATHER CARMODY AND MR. KIN-
cade had conferred in the old priest's
room in Holy Cross House. Under other circumstances, it
might have been a joyful reunion, but Mr. Kincade was concerned about his sons.

"They're no more guilty than I am."

"Of murder."

A faint smile. "Thank you for taking care of the Corby
statue incident, Father."

"I had had practice. Have you spoken to the boys?"

"My main concern has been to find a good local lawyer.
Some sort of charge will be brought against them. And rightly
so."

Fauxhall, whatever private doubts he might have, was pro-
ceeding on the basis of the veracity of Malcolm Kincade's
claim to have killed Madeline. Jimmy Stewart tried to dissuade
the assistant prosecutor by pointing out that the boy gave a
very vague description of how he had killed the woman. Fauxhall demanded that the other twin be arrested, and he had
been. Now Jimmy was once more a frequent presence at the
Tranquil Motel, interviewing everybody one more time.

Maria Concepción seemed to have forgotten any English she knew, and Kitty, the bookkeeper, acted as translator.

"I had hoped to be a missionary," Kitty explained. "To Latin America."

Her dream had been to rescue the huddled masses in the Southern Hemisphere from the superstition of Romanism, something she said as if Jimmy would agree. There was a Spanish edition of the Bible on the bookkeeper's desk. Her mood was not improved by the rosary that Maria Concepción twisted in her fingers while she looked at Jimmy with wide and fearful eyes. Jimmy wanted to hear again just what Maria Concepción and Rosita had come upon in the bedroom of suite 302 last Monday. Kitty's translation was much longer than the frightened woman's answer.

Kitty explained. "She's afraid you'll send her home."

The bookkeeper's description of the scene was more helpful. She had accompanied Michael Beatty to the suite after the cleaning ladies had spread the alarm.

"Why do people act as if God's law did not apply to motels?" Kitty asked. "The things that go on here."

"Madeline O'Toole certainly had quite a time here."

Kitty's eyes closed as if in pain. "And then to find that the woman wrote filthy novels."

"Well, novels."

"Filthy novels. She left one in the bar when she dragged that bearded man back to her lair. Phyllis passed it on to me." Kitty opened a drawer of her desk and brought out a gaudy paperback. She held it by a corner of its cover before dropping it on the desk. *Dancing in Charleston!*"

"Did you read it?"

"Enough to see the kind of thing it is."

"I'd better take that."

"Please." Kitty pushed the book toward him.

Michael Beatty was more wary. "How long is this going to go on?"

"Until it's over. "

"But that boy confessed."

"We're going to need more than his word that he did it."

Annoying people at the Tranquil Motel at least kept Jimmy away from Fauxhall. The assistant prosecutor felt that he was being made a public fool of. The collapse of his case against Magnus O'Toole followed by the theatrical confession of Malcolm Kincade had undermined Fauxhall's sense that he was a serious man engaged in a serious profession.

Despite his determination to take the Kincade twins seriously, he had refused to let Quintin Kelly return to Athens, Georgia. "He is a material witness."

"What did he witness?" Crumley asked.

"Would you prefer that I make him a suspect?"

"You wouldn't dare."

But in his present mood Crumley was not sure. The upshot was that he would agree, as a professional courtesy to the prosecutor's office, to keep his client in the vicinity and available. That meant the condo where Kelly and O'Toole were still ensconced.

"You didn't tell me that Madeline had left one of her novels in the bar," Jimmy said to Phyllis Brickhouse.

"She didn't. She gave it to me."

"And you gave it to Kitty."

Phyllis smirked. "She sits in there crunching numbers, convinced that this place is Sodom and whatchamacallit. I thought she'd like a little proof."

"Tell me about the Kincade boy."

"What a doll." Her smile faded. "What more can I tell you? He came in, he had a few drinks, he recognized the woman and sat at her table with the bearded guy. I've told you all this. I told your assistant."

"My assistant?"

"The boy cop. Larry something."

"Douglas!"

"Larry Douglas. That's right. He said he had gone to St. Joe."

"After your time."

"His fiancée came in." Phyllis made a face. "I thought you had to be in shape to be a cop."

Jimmy took another look at suite 302, which was still marked off as a crime scene. He would have been better advised to sit at his desk and study the list of things they had taken out of the suite. But that would have put him in range of Fauxhall. He called campus security and told Larry Douglas he was coming out.

"Any help I can be, Stewart."

Phyllis's remark had brought back to Jimmy the conversation he had had with Casey in the courthouse cafeteria that morning. Casey sauntered around the courthouse as if he owned the place, which was not far from the truth.

"You know a kid named Larry Douglas?" he asked Jimmy.

"What's he done?"

"Ho ho. Feeney in the coroner's office thinks he'd make a good cop."

"He's already on campus security at Notre Dame."

"He wants to be a real cop."

"It's better than working."

"Ho ho. He thought you'd write a recommendation for him."

"Who, Feeney?"

Casey was out of ho hos. "I'd consider it a favor."

Jimmy had agreed, for what good it would do Douglas. If Casey wanted him on the force, he would get on the force.

Douglas was waiting for him outside the entrance of campus security.

"I thought you'd want to talk in private."

They crossed the road to the eatery in Grace Hall, taking their coffee to one of the outside tables. It was a beautiful day, the trees turning, sunny, students hurrying in dozens of directions.

"So how is the investigation going?"

"I thought you'd want to report to me. Phyllis Brickhouse told me you were at the Tranquil Motel impersonating a cop."

"I dropped by, sure. We talked. She thought I was a cop?" Larry's smile rounded his cheeks, and his eyes lit up.

"Casey tells me you want to join the force."

Larry was overjoyed. He owed it to Feeney, he knew that, although he hadn't been sure that the assistant coroner would deliver on his promise to intercede for him with Casey.

"You probably have better perks on the Notre Dame payroll."

"I'm being wasted here."

"Will your girlfriend stay here?"

"Where else would she go? Bring me up to speed on the investigation."

"Well, we have a confession."

"The Kincade boy? You think he did it?"

"I wonder who fed Grafton all that crap? You didn't talk to him, did you?"

"I've been thinking, Stewart. What if it was an inside job?"

"How do you mean?"

"A theft! Do we know what was missing from that suite? Look, that place is crawling with illegals. Say one of them was caught rifling through the lady's things. She panics, thinking she'll be exported. There is a struggle . . ."

"You have anyone in mind?"

"How about those cleaning ladies?"

"How about Phyllis Brickhouse? How about the manager?"

"You don't like the idea."

"It's no dumber than the one I'm pursuing."

"Rufus James?"

5 BENJAMIN EVANS HAD LOCATED the bearded man who was Rufus James in a motel in Dowagiac, Michigan, after hours of patient phone calls to motels in the area. But it was a clean-shaven Rufus James who came to the door of the unit when Jimmy showed up with the local sheriff. He just looked at Jimmy when he said he'd like to have a few words with him.

"What is this? I'm working."

"It's about the murder at the Tranquil Motel in South Bend last Sunday."

"I don't know what you're talking about."

"You were seen there last weekend. I thought you might be able to help in our investigation."

"You're kidding."

"You spent time with the murdered woman in the motel bar Saturday night. She took you to her room."

"What are you, the morals squad?"

"No. Homicide. What I would suggest, Mr. James, is that you agree to come back to South Bend with me, acting just as a dutiful citizen, to be of what help you can."

"And if I don't?"

Jimmy showed him the warrant Fauxhall had been almost eager to have made out.

The assistant prosecutor was losing faith that the Kincade twins were the solution to his problem. "I'll nail them for something, by God. You don't make a mockery of the law with impunity." Meanwhile, Fauxhall thought it would help if they could talk to the other bearded man.

"I do this under protest," James said.

"Just so you do it."

Jimmy thanked the sheriff and headed back to South Bend with a silent Rufus James, wondering if the man in the passenger seat was the murderer they sought.

"You shaved."

"After puberty, it becomes a habit."

"How much have you read about the killing?"

"Look, I've been holed up in that motel for days, writing."

"All the witnesses commented on your beard."

"Maybe I'll let it grow again."

"Prisoners often do."

"What the hell does that mean?"

"Just an observation."

Interrogations have a logic of their own, but it is seldom sequential, going from point A to point B; rather, circuitously, off on one or another apparent tangent suggested by an answer or sometimes just a facial reaction, the exchange meanders on. Rufus James proved to be an interesting subject.

His status as a writer was obviously most important to him,

and not just any sort of writer, as Jimmy discovered when he observed that the victim, too, had been an author.

James snorted. "Do you know her stuff?"

"She told me all about it."

"You weren't impressed."

"What is my opinion against that of hundreds of thousands?"

"A lot better?"

Jimmy got a little disquisition on the nature of true literature. James made it sound like a religion of which he was one of the high priests. "I don't suppose you know my novel."

"Tell me about it."

"You wouldn't like it."

"What is my opinion against that of hundreds of thousands?"

"Ha. I doubt that ten thousand people have read my novel." He didn't seem to be complaining. "The Revolt of the Masses took over publishing decades ago. The way that woman described her writing! She just sits down and the story comes. 'I feel as if I'm taking dictation.'" He seemed to be mimicking Madeline's voice. "I suppose that is the great difference. Some books are written, others are dictated. Meaning that the writer is simply listening to all the echoes of the stuff she has read."

"The bartender thought the two of you got along very well."

"Madeline was an appetizing creature."

James observed a moment of silence. He didn't pretend to be grieving.

"And then you were interrupted by a young man named Kincade."

"It's amazing. I came north to get away from the South, so I could write about it, and I found myself surrounded by Johnny Rebs. The sentimental South. Pure myth, of course."

"So the two of you went off to her suite."

James looked at him.

"No comment?"

"You seem to know all about it."

"This is my job. You realize that, don't you? I'm not prying into your personal life."

"Just asking if I went to bed with that woman?"

"Did you?"

"Of course. It seemed the path of least resistance."

"Did you resist?"

"Not really."

"And again you were interrupted by young Kincade."

"He was feeling no pain. He wanted to apologize for interrupting us before by interrupting us again."

"You went off with him."

"It was a way to get away. Besides, he offered to give me a lift."

"Did he?"

"I had a car. A rental."

"What are you writing now?"

"A novel."

"A Southern novel?"

"What do you know about the Underground Railroad?"

"Tell me."

"It's what they called the path runaway slaves took north. Dowagiac was a station on that railway."

"Tell me about last Sunday."

"I thought we were talking about Saturday."

"Madeline O'Toole was killed on Sunday. A bearded man was seen at the motel. A bearded man the witness connected with Saturday. Why did you shave off your beard?"

"Have you ever grown a beard?"

"No."

"Don't. They're a damned nuisance."

"Did you return to the motel on Sunday?"

"Yes."

The answer surprised Jimmy. Surely the fellow got the drift of these questions? "What time?"

"It was afternoon."

"Madeline O'Toole was killed on Sunday afternoon."

"I know. She was dead when I let myself into the suite. I had taken the plastic key when I offered to get rid of the boy, telling her I would be back. Once outside, I decided to get back to Michigan."

"But you returned to the motel on Sunday afternoon?"

"Yes. When I realized she was dead, I just got out of there."

"Have you any idea what your story sounds like?"

"Tell me."

"A work of fiction."

6 AND SO THE MURDER OF MADE-
line O'Toole seemed solved. Jimmy
brought the good news to the Knight apartment, and he and
Phil went over what Jimmy had learned, both of them as jubilant as professional detectives ever get. Roger sat at the great
trestle table on which they dined, papers spread before him:
transcripts of interrogations, the list of things taken from the
motel suite, the coroner's report, copies of the series Grafton
had written when Malcolm Kincade had seemed the culprit, a
copy of *Dixie Coup*. When Jimmy looked at the cover photograph of the author, he said, "That's the way he looks now. A
little older, of course."

"Why do you suppose he admitted returning to the motel on
Sunday?" Roger asked.

"I told him we had a witness."

"No wonder he shaved off his beard."

"He wouldn't have known that then."

"He would have known that he could have been seen."

"I suppose."

Rufus James's fingerprints were everywhere in the suite—
in the sitting room, in the bedroom, in the bathroom.

"What would have been his motive?" Roger asked.

Phil turned to his brother. "You heard Jimmy, Roger. This guy thinks of himself as a Nobel Prize winner, an artist."

"So?"

"So in his cups he told Madeline that he was a hack as well. My guess is that when he remembered that, he wanted to correct the impression. Or shut her up. What would happen to the reputation of the author of *Dixie Coup* if she blabbed all over the place that James wrote thrillers? And she did blab."

"I'd like to talk to him."

"That's all right with me," Jimmy said.

An hour later Roger was seated across from Rufus James in a visiting room in the city jail. James had been somewhat taken aback when he was led into the room and saw Roger trying to get comfortable in a chair.

"Who are you?"

"One of your readers."

James sat down. "An exclusive club."

"I won't say that I enjoyed *Dixie Coup*."

"I hope not. Literature should not be read for enjoyment."

"An interesting theory."

"Let's just say that I'm an acquired taste."

"You're accused of killing Madeline O'Toole."

James sighed. "Do you know a lawyer named Crumley? He's offered to represent me."

"I don't know him. You will need a lawyer."

"Detective Stewart said my story sounds like fiction."

"Is it?"

"Only the fictional parts."

"And what are they?"

"I told him the Underground Railroad figures in my new novel."

"You also told him you came north in order to write about the South."

"That is true."

"That you told him?"

James smiled. "Are you a detective or what?"

"I thought you'd never ask. I'm a professor at Notre Dame. Roger Knight."

"I went to Notre Dame. What a place it was in those days. Frank O'Malley, John T. Frederick, John Edward Hardy, John Logan." James said the names as if he were reciting the litany of the saints. "They made me want to be a writer."

"Did you go to the game last Saturday?"

James smiled sardonically. "I never went to a single game when I was a student. But last week I made a little pilgrimage to campus. Everyone was excited about the coming game, and I thought I might go. As a lark. I drove down on Saturday. Do you know what I was asked to pay for a ticket?"

"So you decided to watch the game in the bar of the Tranquil Motel."

"How could I resist a place with a name like that?"

"And you met Madeline O'Toole."

"A terribly mixed-up woman. When she said she was from Memphis, I understood."

"She was a writer."

James hesitated. "I suppose I should speak well of the dead."

"But not of her fiction?"

"I am sure it could be read with enjoyment," James said wryly.

"You told her that you are the author of many thrillers."

James sat back. "How did you know that?"

"She spread the good news."

He thought about it for a moment, then smiled. "Fame at last."

"It doesn't bother you?"

"Why should it? Some people might be impressed."

"Why would you tell her something like that?"

James studied Roger. "I don't know how well versed you are in the art of seduction."

"I am not even well prosed."

"Very good. Anyway, it seemed a way to her heart. And so it was. We toddled off to bed as fellow hacks."

"And you returned on Sunday."

"Lust is a tyrannical vice. The lady and I had had a pleasant time. An aesthetic personality always imagines that repetition is possible."

"Kierkegaard."

"What do you teach?"

"I am the Huneker Professor of Catholic Studies."

"Good Lord."

"Tell me about Sunday afternoon."

"No need to describe the heated anticipation with which I

drove from Dowagiac. I arrived, parked, let myself in by the north door, and hurried to the suite. When I had left the night before, I took the door key with me, thinking I would be right back. It enabled me to enter the suite without needing to knock. I found the body in the bedroom."

"What was your first thought?"

"Flight."

And fly he had, or drive, putting miles between himself and the grim scene in that motel bedroom. The beard? Of course he had feared someone might have seen him there. He did not want to get mixed up in that kind of mess.

"And now you are."

"Stewart was right. This does sound like fiction. Madeline O'Toole fiction."

"I think you're telling the truth."

"Thank you."

Roger got to his feet with an effort that Rufus James observed from a seated position. He turned his clean-shaven face up to Roger.

"Help me."

(7)   THE KINCADES, FATHER, SONS, AND daughter, along with Caleb Lanier, were having dinner at Papa Vino's in Mishawaka. The twins were subdued, having spent several hours in conference with Crumley, the lawyer, who seemed pessimistic about their chances of walking off scot-free. He would not be representing them at their disciplinary hearing at Notre Dame, but that was the least of their worries.

"They'll throw you out," Mr. Kincade said. The thought did not seem to sadden him. "They should have thrown me out. Well, maybe Father Carmody can work his magic for you, too."

"We can transfer to Georgia Tech."

"And be scratched by cheerleaders."

Sarah thought that her brothers were safe now that the man who had killed Madeline O'Toole was under arrest. She actually beamed at her brothers, full of admiration. She said that they reminded her of the twins in *Gone with the Wind*.

"Weren't they killed?"

"Oh, shut up."

Malcolm told his father that Caleb was the guilty one. He

had written a story praising Father Corby's role as a Union chaplain in the Civil War.

"He was a brave man."

"That's all Caleb meant to say." Sarah patted his hand.

Malcom reached for the carafe of wine, and his father stayed his hand. "You're on the water wagon, son."

"I was going to toast Father Corby."

"Well, in that case."

Glasses were raised in honor of the third president of Notre Dame. Caleb proposed another, to John Bannister Tabb.

"Good boy," Mr. Kincade said. "I'll drink to that."

They all did.

They went on to drink to Caleb's namesake Sidney Lanier, fellow prisoner of Tabb. Musicians both, but it was Lanier who, after the war, thought back sadly to the wild emotions with which he and others had marched off to battle. With experience, the resonant abstract words had given way to grimmer realities, and soldiers in the field tried to forget the endless political arguments that continued in the cities, besieged and unbesieged, behind them. At times there seemed more camaradie between the boys facing one another in opposite trenches than between either army and its wrangling civilians.

"There were civil wars on both sides in the Civil War," Mr. Kincade intoned, and earned disappointed glances from his sons. Caleb said to Sarah that they must bring her father around to meet Roger Knight.

"I apologized to the man whose truck I stole," Malcolm said.

"That may help you with Father Carmody," said the father.

"Jackson," Malcom said. "Do you know what his nickname is?"

"Jackson's?"

"Yes." Malcolm looked around the table brightly. "Stonewall!"

8 ⟶ ROGER RETURNED FROM TALKING
with Rufus James in a pensive mood and
gave only half an ear to the conversation going on between his
brother and Jimmy Stewart. The tone of their voices conveyed
the satisfaction they felt that they could consider the murder
or homicide—Fauxhall had still not made up his mind what
charge to bring against James—of Madeline O'Toole solved.
Roger sat at the trestle table, shuffling through all the papers
that were still there. It was when he was studying the list of
items taken from suite 302 at the Tranquil Motel that the
thought came. He sat back, his massive face seeming to
reflect the sorting out that was going on in his head. The
voices in the room became inaudible.

Roger rose slowly, put on a great hooded jacket, and shuf-
fled to the door. "I'm going out."

Phil turned, distracted. "Where?"

"The Tranquil Motel."

He rode the wave of laughter into the great outdoors.

It was later afternoon now, gathering dusk, and what he
proposed to do was doubly dangerous, driving through the twi-
light in his golf cart. But he thought not so much of the journey ahead as of its goal. Before turning the key in his golf cart,

he got out his cell phone and made the call that told him his journey would not be in vain.

A golf cart was all very well on the roads and walks of campus, but once Roger had gone through the gate and headed north, he had to find less traveled roads, and he found them, parallel to 31. When he crossed Cleveland, he continued north for half a mile and then saw his way clear to head west. The twinkling sign of the motel was visible through the gloaming.

Some minutes later, he pulled up at the entrance of the motel and began the great struggle to get out of the cart and onto his feet. The doors of the motel slid open at his approach, and when he came into the lobby, heads turned at the apparition. Roger's bulky figure looked as if he weighed more than three hundred pounds because of his open jacket. He flung back the hood, lumbered to the desk, and told the startled clerk that he wished to see Miss Callendar.

"Kitty?"

"I called twenty minutes ago."

"I am the manager, Michael Beatty. Can I help you?"

"Yes, you can. Take me to Kitty Callendar."

Beatty hesitated, as if he thought he should forewarn Kitty of this unusual visitor, but he came around the desk and led Roger down the hall, calling "Kitty, Kitty," as they went. All Beatty lacked was a saucer of milk.

Kitty Callendar sat behind her desk, back firm against the back of her chair, her gathered hair pinned atop her head, a manhattan on the desk before her. On the monitor of her computer, from which she had turned when Roger appeared in her doorway, the logo of the motel changed positions on the screen.

"I telephoned," Roger said.

"Are you the one who asked if I was still here?"

"The same."

"Come in."

Easier said than done, as it happened. A frontal assault pinned Roger's shoulders to the sides of the door, but by turning sideways and with an assist from Beatty he managed to squeeze inside. "Thank you," Roger said sweetly but dismissively, and Beatty backed off down the hall.

"I would ask you to sit down, but . . ."

Roger smiled. "I can stand, thank you. My name is Roger Knight. You will have talked with my brother, Philip, who has been assisting Jimmy Stewart investigating the unfortunate death of Madeline O'Toole in this motel last weekend."

"The terrible publicity was deserved," Kitty said, chin up. "The things that go on in this motel!" She picked up her glass and sipped. "Adults are bad enough, but when you have a middle-aged woman seducing a boy!"

"I suppose you notice everything."

"Have I any choice? I would have to be dumb and blind not to notice."

"They have arrested a man and will charge him with homicide at least."

"Let us hope that this time they have the right one."

"I don't think they do."

She sat more upright. "Really?"

"It was while studying the list of things taken from the suite in which the woman died that it struck me that you are the key to this whole sad business."

"I have cooperated as best I can."

Roger's hand rested on the Spanish Bible on the desktop, as if he were about to take an oath. He looked at what his hand rested on, then picked it up. "Spanish?"

"My great desire was to be a missionary." She peered at Roger. "Your brother assured me that he is not a Roman."

"Catholic? Oh, no. I'm the Catholic one."

"Good heavens. Well, I hope you are ashamed of the behavior of your coreligionists. Imagine that woman, after a night of riot, going off to church with the boy she had led astray."

"Well, her name was Madeline."

"Mary Magdalene? She was a repentant sinner."

"Let us hope that unfortunate woman was, too. At the last."

"Far from it!"

"You were there, weren't you?"

"What do you mean?"

"It is so easy to overlook the small, significant thing. You lost some of your hairpins when you struggled with that woman."

"Struggled with her?"

"Killed her."

Silence in the office. On the computer screen the motel logo changed positions.

"That's nonsense."

"Women do not use hairpins anymore. They are rarer than hair combs. But you need pins to keep your hair in that style, don't you? My Aunt Agatha did."

"Please get out of this office."

Roger was digging in his pocket for his cell phone when she came around the desk, heading right at him like a woman with a mission. He backed up toward the door and a moment later was in the doorway.

"Let me by."

"I'm afraid I'm stuck."

She pushed at him, but this only wedged him more tightly in the doorway. The fear that had begun when he mentioned the hairpins was now bright in her eyes. She began to beat on Roger's chest.

His hand was on his cell phone now, and he felt the vibration that he preferred to a ring. He took out the phone. "Phil?"

"Roger, where are you?"

"Where I said I was going. The Tranquil Motel. Get here as quickly as you can. And bring Jimmy."

Kitty followed this conversation angrily. Again she pushed at Roger, trying to dislodge him from the doorway. She beat on his chest in frustration. And then, with preternatural calm, she returned to her desk, where she finished her drink and picked up her Bible. She was still reading it when Phil and Jimmy arrived.

PART FIVE

1   DESPITE FATHER CARMODY'S IN-
tercession, the Kincade twins were sent
home for a semester's probation. This would postpone their
graduation until the summer after their class graduated, but
they would be retained on the roll of that year. Mr. Kincade
found this an agreeable compromise.

The football season ended, midsemester came and went,
and one February day, Caleb Lanier and Sarah Kincade were
walking hand in hand on one of the lake paths. Any timidity
Caleb had felt with Sarah was long since gone. She freed her
hand, stooped, and filled her mittens with snow, trying to
make a ball, but it was not wet enough. So she just rubbed the
snow in Caleb's face and then set off down the path on the
run. He caught up with her, and they tumbled together in the
snow. He looked down into her taunting, laughing face.

"Sarah, *te amavi*," he said.

"What?"

"It's Augustinian. Roger Knight suggested it."

"What does it mean?"

"We must ask him."

When they did ask the Huneker Professor of Catholic Studies he became sheepish. "I hope it isn't sacrilegious."

"Tell me!"

He got out the *Confessions* and found the line and read it aloud. *Sero te amavi.*

"What does it mean?"

"Late have I loved thee." Roger actually blushed. "Of course, Augustine was addressing God, so the use I suggested to Caleb was perhaps inappropriate, but . . ."

Sarah interrupted him by throwing her arms about Roger. Or as about him as his girth and the length of her arms permitted.

Roger made popcorn then, and hot chocolate, and they settled down at the trestle table. Phil was in a beanbag chair in the next room, napping before the television, where a muted basketball game was on.

"Tell us again how you knew it was Kitty Callendar who had killed Madeline O'Toole," Sarah urged.

"How I pinned the crime on her?" He tried to duck her playful punch.

Fauxhall had shown little confidence when Jimmy presented him with the basis for charging Kitty Callendar with the murder of Madeline O'Toole. "That's all you've got?"

It was more than enough for Crumley, who successfully demanded that his client be released. But of course physical evidence is always incommensurate with the crime it points to. If Kitty Callendar had not decided to take pride in what she had done, the case would doubtless have seemed flimsy. Where outside of a detective novel would three hairpins spell Q.E.D.? But Kitty had decided that she had acted as an agent of the divine wrath.

"Would Abraham have been guilty of murder if he had slain Isaac?"

It said something of her state of mind that she found this a relevant parallel. By that time, in fact, her lawyer, a shrewd local attorney named Alex Cholis, had decided to enter a plea of innocent because of insanity.

"I am not insane," Kitty said to her lawyer.

"Well, you're not innocent, either, are you?"

The plea made Fauxhall's work much simpler, and there was little doubt that Kitty would spend some years undergoing therapy, a severer punishment perhaps than life imprisonment or even execution. Not that either of those would have been in the offing.

Roger's course in the spring semester was devoted to Ambrose Bierce.

"What has he got to do with Notre Dame?" Phil asked.

"Not much, but he fought in an Indiana regiment."

Bierce's haunting stories of the Civil War, rather than *The Devil's Dictionary*, were the focus of the course. But it was the way Bierce's life had ended, or seemed to end, when he mysteriously disappeared into Mexico that fascinated Roger.

"Just faded away?" Caleb asked.

There are worse ways for a story to end.